ROCK SOLID

A ROCK SOLID CONSTRUCTION NOVEL

BY RILEY HART

Published by

Riley Hart

Cover Design by X-Potion Designs

Cover Photo by jackson photografix

Dedication:

To Dawn Martin Frakes—thank you for naming Rockford Falls. It's the perfect home for this series.

Also, this book is dedicated to anyone who suffers from the devastating disease that is addiction. You are strong. You can overcome it. There is a beautiful life out there for you, waiting for you to live it.

CHAPTER ONE

Trevor Dixon looked across the desk at his younger-by-six-minutes brother. His dark brown hair lay flat on his head, reminding Trevor that he hadn't combed his own this morning. He didn't much get the point. It wasn't as if his fingers didn't run through it a million times a day. Plus, they worked construction for God's sake. They wore hard hats most of the time, their hair either wet with sweat or the water they poured over themselves to keep cool.

Still, today, Trevor and Blake's hair each behaved much in the same way as Trevor and Blake themselves, in that Blake behaved...and Trevor didn't.

Trevor scratched the side of his head, where it was buzzed shorter than the couple inches it was on the top.

"How you doing, big brother?" Blake asked him. It was a simple enough question, and Trevor knew that he only asked because he cared, but it still grated on his nerves.

It wasn't a *how you doing today,* kind of question. It was a *you're not having the urge to drink, right?* question.

"Rock solid." Trevor grinned at his brother, who laughed.

"Pun intended, right?" Rockford Falls. It's where they'd lived most of their lives. Trevor left to get clean, and he was in San Francisco a lot when he wasn't clean, but for Blake, Rockford had always been home. Add in the fact that they were co-owners of a new construction company, Rock Solid Construction—yeah, the pun had been intended.

"You're hilarious," Blake added.

"I try hard. So, what do we have for today?"

"It's the last week on the library. JT, Jason, and Andrea are already on their way out. We have to meet them there. We're going to have to take two trucks, though. I got a call for an estimate this morning. It's a remodel out at the old Stoneridge property. I didn't know someone bought it, did you?"

Before Trevor could reply, his brother continued. "Anyway, could be a good job, which we need. I'd like to be able to keep JT and Andrea on after the library, but it depends on what we can land. I'd really like to remodel that house. It's fucking gorgeous. Plus, there's no doubt the money could be good. I figured I'd go out and meet with the guy. You can head over to the library and then I'll meet you out there when I'm done."

"Why don't you let me go?" Trevor asked.

Blake paused. It was a shitty feeling to know his baby brother didn't trust him to be able to close a deal. It wasn't that Trevor didn't get it, either. He'd fucked up a lot in his life. Fucked up badly. But that was in the past. He was getting his shit together now. He'd been clean for one year, one month, and three days. They were running a business together now, or trying to. Trevor could handle this.

"Blake, if this is going to work, you have to trust me. What do you think I'm going to do? Stop and get a beer on the way? I could do that just as easily on my way to the job site if I wanted to."

"No. Hell no. That's not it." Blake shook his head, but Trevor knew it kind of *was* it. At least partially.

"I can't only do the heavy lifting. I have to be able to do both parts of the business. What if you're sick or, hell, what if you want to go on vacation sometime? I can do it. I can nail this." Because they *really* needed the work. Things were slow since they were just starting up. They were lucky to have enough work that they needed JT and Andrea right now. If they wanted to keep Blake's friends on, they needed to get more jobs lined up.

It wouldn't matter if they had no work at all, Jason would always be around. He and Blake were inseparable. They had been for years. But Andrea and JT…they couldn't make the two of them any promises, but Trevor wanted to do his best by them.

"Yeah, okay. You go get this job and I'll go work my ass off at the job site. I see your plan." Blake winked at him and Trevor grinned.

His brother had every reason not to trust Trevor. Most people he knew had every reason not to trust him, but Blake was his twin. No matter what had gone down, they were always close. They read each other, and understood each other in ways most people didn't. In a lot of ways, they were the same person, even though Blake always did the right thing and Trevor often did the wrong one.

Even when Trevor started going off the rails, drowning in a bottle like their father did, Blake never turned his back on him. He told Trevor when Trevor was fucking up, but he'd never turned his back on him, even when Trevor probably deserved it.

If anyone believed in him, it would be his brother.

"Thanks, bro." They both stood and Trevor gave him a half hug, patting him on the back.

"No problem. You go get this job for us, okay? You got this. I know it."

"I know." This time it was Trevor who winked at Blake. He would do this. He would land this job, and they would keep Rock Solid afloat. They would thrive and Trevor would stay clean. He'd make everything up to them, and maybe even deserve the second chance he'd been given.

***

Simon Malone opened and closed his right hand over and over again. It was stiff, though it always was now. He didn't have all the feeling in it that he should, though he had more than he used to.

It wasn't enough. The stiffness, the lack of feeling, the lack of control wouldn't work for him. Couldn't be a very good surgeon if your hand didn't work properly. He couldn't be a surgeon at all, not anymore. Still, Simon opened and closed his hand as though the simple exercise would suddenly change things. As though the feeling would suddenly come back, and the shaking wouldn't be a problem. Like he would be the man he used to be, the decorated cardio-thoracic surgeon with the magic hands.

Before he could start his day too pissy, Simon pushed out of his kitchen chair and went to fill up his glass of orange juice. If he didn't do something to take his mind off his lack of career, there would be no coming back from his bad mood. He'd bite the head off of the construction worker when he arrived, which would screw up his plans for today of figuring out who could help him remodel the house the way he wanted. It gave him something to do, planning this remodel, and it wasn't like he could do the work himself.

Who was he kidding, though? Simon was a miserable bastard, and regardless of getting his mind off his hand, he'd be an asshole to whoever came to the door.

He poured his drink and stood in the kitchen, gulping it down in quick swallows.

Once it was finished, Simon washed the glass. As he set it on the rack to dry, the doorbell rang.

Finally.

He glanced at his watch and then went to the door. "You're late." Five minutes, but still.

"I'm sorry about that. It's been a while since I've come out this way. The driveway is a little overgrown and I missed it." The brown-haired man ran a hand through his hair before holding it out to Simon. He had a tattoo from elbow to wrist on his right arm—a skull and something else. Simon would never understand that, marking your body that way. He had a dark brown beard that matched his hair. It wasn't thick, just a few days' worth of growth, neatly trimmed, and damned if he didn't have a stud in his bottom lip. Ridiculous. "I'm Trevor Dixon from Rock Solid Construction. I appreciate you giving us a chance to come out here and see what you need done. I think you'll find we're the right people for the job."

Simon couldn't tell if the man was simply that confident or if he just wanted to come off that way.

They shook hands, and Simon immediately had the most ridiculous thought… *Can he feel it? Can he tell my hand is fucked up just from touching it?*

Simon pulled back. It was a crazy thing to think. He knew that. And in most activities, he was fine. Yeah, there was pain, but he could handle that. Every day activities and repairing hearts were two different things.

"If you'll follow me. The work needs to be done on the main house." Simon stepped out of the guesthouse and closed the door. "I want a pretty hefty remodel. The upstairs especially. I need a wall knocked out between two of the upstairs rooms to make one. One of the rooms will become a library, so I'll need shelves on all the walls—"

"A library?" Trevor asked. Simon sensed interest in the construction worker's voice.

"Yes," was his only reply. He wanted a medical library. Eventually, he would write a book on the heart.

They made their way to the house. Simon showed the other man around, giving him ideas of everything he wanted done. Walls knocked down here, new walls there. He wanted the layout of the downstairs slightly changed.

Trevor, Simon thought his name was, asked questions here and there. He wrote down close to everything that Simon said.

"Great. This sounds like it's going to be a beauty when we're done with it." Trevor winked at Simon and he realized the man *was* playing him. He wanted Simon to think he was confident so that Simon would give them the job. He wasn't stupid, though. Rock Solid wasn't the only place he called.

"The timeframe might be pushing it a little bit. We'll need permits. We'll also have to look into a few contractors we work with on electrical, but I can give you more specifics after I sit down with my co-owner. We'll draw up some plans and get a quote going for you—shit!"

Simon turned to look at the construction worker, who held his hand.

"What happened?" Simon asked just as blood started to slide through Trevor's fingers.

"Nothing. It's okay."

Great. The construction worker cut his hand before Simon had even decided if he wanted to give the man the job or not. That couldn't be a good sign.

"Let me see it," he said. "And what did you cut it on?"

"Nothing. It's okay. It's not bad. My mistake. Either myself or Blake will call you in a day or so with more information."

Simon reached out and grabbed Trevor's hand. His vision swam a little, not because he had a problem with blood but because he had a problem with injured hands.

"It's deep. You need stitches."

"No, it's okay. I—"

"It's not," Simon cut him off, just as he saw a nail, the end broken off, sticking out of the wall. At least he knew the culprit. He added a tetanus shot to things Trevor might need. “Let’s go inside. We need to wrap it up to stop the bleeding and then get you to the ER for stitches.”

A hospital. The one place he didn’t want to go again, yet the place he used to consider home. This day was shaping up to be a real doozy.

CHAPTER TWO

The tone of Simon's voice told Trevor the man definitely wasn't happy about having to do this. Welcome to the fucking club. Trevor wasn't either. What he really wanted to do was tell Simon to pull the stick out of his ass and relax. Oh, and Trevor could get *himself* to the hospital, thank you very much, but he managed to bite his tongue. Telling the guy off wasn't the best way to get this job.

Not that he probably had a chance now. Ripping his hand open on a nail sticking out of the wall wasn't the best way to show the guy how capable he was.

Perfect. Just perfect. Blake would be understanding about it like he always was, but Trevor knew what he'd be thinking—that if he'd gone himself, this wouldn't have happened.

And he'd be right.

Simon's steps were quick as he led Trevor back to the other house. If his hand wasn't bleeding all over the damn place, Trevor would take the time to admire the man's ass. It was tight, sexy, but definitely nice handfuls to grab ahold of. Too bad he was an uptight prick.

Simon's movements were smooth as he cleaned Trevor's hand and wrapped it with gauze and tape from a first-aid kit. Either Simon cut himself a lot, or he had experience. Not that it surprised him. The guy reeked of money, and a holier-than-thou attitude. It would make sense if he was in the medical field.

"Really, I can drive myself to the hospital. It's a cut on my hand."

"No. It's my responsibility. It happened on my property," he said tensely.

Shit. "You don't have to worry about that." They definitely weren't getting the job now. The guy felt like he had to pay for Trevor's injury. And maybe technically he was supposed to, but it was Trevor's dumbass mistake, not paying attention. That was important to him now, taking responsibility for his own actions.

"Actually, I do. My car is this way." He looked at Trevor like he was an idiot.

Don't hit him, don't hit him, don't hit him, Trevor repeated in his head. It was an easy way to handle conflicts before. Things were different now. He was a twenty-five year old man. He could and would take care of himself. Still, he didn't want to screw this up more than he already had, so Trevor followed Mr. Stick-Up-His-Ass to the car, wishing like hell he could tell Simon a dick was a lot more fun.

They were silent the whole way to the hospital. When they got to the Emergency Room, Simon walked up the counter. "I'm Dr. Simon Malone, part of the cardiac team at Roosevelt Heart and Vascular Institute in San Francisco. We had a little accident on my property. Mr..."

Simon turned his determined eyes on Trevor.

"Dixon," he supplied his last name for the second time.

"Mr. Dixon cut the palm of his hand pretty bad. It's going to need stitches."

"I'll let the nurse know, Dr. Malone, and they'll get him right back." The receptionist scampered to the back.

"You shouldn't have done that. I can wait like everyone else." Shit like that pissed Trevor off; *Dr. Malone,* throwing his title around like he was more important than everyone else.

Trevor ignored the throb in his hand as Simon raised a brow at him. Of course. This wasn't about Trevor. It was Simon who couldn't wait.

"Why don't you go? I'll have someone pick me up. I don't need anyone here holding my hand. As far as I'm concerned, this didn't even happen on your property."

"Mr. Dixon, we have a room for you." The receptionist stuck her head out of the sliding door.

Before Trevor said anything, Simon was walking back. Trevor really had no choice except to follow him, and his hand hurt like a bitch.

They'd probably give him some good....fuck. He couldn't take anything. He wouldn't. Drinking might have been his gateway, but there had been plenty of pills that followed it, and other drugs behind the pills. The last thing he needed was to get any of that shit in his system again.

Trevor squeezed his eyes shut. *My job, Blake, Mom...* He thought about the things he had in his life that were important to him. The things he risked losing if he screwed up.

He wouldn't fuck this up. No matter what. He was doing this. One day at a time. That's what they told him in his classes. One day at a time.

***

A registration clerk came back to get all of Trevor's information. Simon watched silently. This part used to bug him sometimes. What he was doing was so much more important, but now, as crazy as it sounded, he actually missed it. Missed the whole process that led a patient to his table. The place where Simon would fix them.

His heart sped up with the memories. The pride that filled him when he saved someone. When he repaired their heart.

"Can I get your insurance information?" The clerk's question snapped Simon out of his memories.

"I'll be covering it. Can you bill me?" he asked.

"No, that's fine. Please, bill me," Trevor said, and Simon's muscles tightened in annoyance.

The young blonde registration clerk's eyes darted back and forth between them as though she didn't know what to do.

"It happened on my property, so I'm responsible," Simon told her.

She nibbled her lip nervously. "I understand that. I've never registered someone that way before. We put spouse or parent information for billing. Other than that it's always insurance or workman's compensation. I…I can try it, though. I mean, if you think I should."

"Jesus Christ," Trevor mumbled, and Simon gave her a smile. Simon liked getting his way.

"Yes, please do."

Trevor wasn't happy about it. The scowl on his face and the thick vein protruding from his forehead made that obvious, but Simon gave his information to the clerk anyway. She finished just as the doctor came in.

"The nurse hasn't been in to see him yet, but I can tell you it's going to need stitches. I cleaned it up before we came in but it's deep, and a good two inches long. Just meat. He didn't knick anything." He'd been able to tell when he cleaned it.

When the older man cocked a brow at him, Simon introduced himself.

"Nice to meet you. I'm Dr. Wells. I did part of my residency in San Francisco, though quite a few years before you, I'm guessing."

"Where?" Simon asked him. Trevor cleared his throat.

"Can we finish up with me please? I have to get back to work."

Simon almost laughed. There would be no work for Trevor. Not with where he cut his hand. Then he was annoyed at himself for laughing because he wasn't in the mood for that. He wanted to talk shop, wanted to breathe in the air of the ER, listen to the hustle of feet and the beep of machines and pretend he was prepping for surgery he would never perform again.

"You can't work," Simon said just as Dr. Wells asked him, "What do you do?"

"Construction, and let me worry about that." Trevor held out his hand for the doctor, who unwrapped it.

A nurse came in and the wound was of course cleaned again, and Dr. Wells examined him. Simon stood off to the side, watching…wishing. He didn't spend a lot of time in the ER, but he still felt close to the job he'd loved so much.

After they finished the examination and the nurse set out supplies, Dr. Wells confirmed from Trevor's paperwork, "You're not allergic to any medications?"

"No."

"We're going to give you a shot for pain. We can send a prescription in for Vicodin afterward. You're going to be sore, and Dr. Malone was right about work."

Trevor's jaw visibly tightened. It looked like he loved his job as much as Simon had.

"I don't want any medication," Trevor gritted out.

"Son, I have to put quite a few stitches in your hand. You're going to need—"

"I refuse. I don't need it. I'll walk out before I let you put drugs in me." Trevor's voice was tight, tighter than Simon had heard it. His eyes were hard on Dr. Wells. Briefly, Trevor glanced his way. It was just a second, but Simon saw it there. The shame.

He was an addict.

Dr. Wells started, "It's not—"

"He has a right to refuse service." He turned to Trevor. "For the record, I'm not sure I agree with you, but you have that right."

This time Trevor's gaze lingered on Simon a little longer. Simon took in the different shades of blue there, how they were darker toward the pupil but got lighter around the edges. *Thank you,* they seemed to say, and Simon gave the man a quick nod.

Dr. Wells sighed but he didn't argue with them anymore.

Simon watched, and quietly critiqued, as Dr. Wells sewed Trevor's meaty palm back together. His hands itched to do that, to take part of a broken human and put it back together again.

But he wouldn't be able to do it. That's what he had to accept. Doctor or not, he would never be able to perform surgery again.

CHAPTER THREE

They'd been silent the whole way back to the doctor's house. Trevor's hand throbbed, pain shooting up his wrist and into his arm. Every bump they hit on the road, he winced but didn't speak.

The doctor knew. He had to. Why else would Trevor have refused pain medicine? Which meant he would worry about Trevor's stability. Questions about Trevor led to questions about Rock Solid. That meant they wouldn't land this job. Andrea and JT would likely be out of work for a while, and Blake would have been right about what Trevor now knew.

Blake should have gone himself.

Even when he wasn't using, Trevor still fucked things up.

"This won't affect the job we can do. I promise you that. We work hard and we get the job done," he said when they pulled into the doctor's driveway.

"Thank you for letting me know." He killed the engine and they got out. Other than the fact that he felt like his hand would fall off, there was no reason Trevor couldn't drive. He retold the doctor everything he'd said earlier about quotes, drawing up plans and getting back to him. Without the doctor saying so, he knew it was useless.

Trevor wanted nothing more than to drive to the small house he shared with his brother, climb into bed and pretend the whole day didn't happen, but he didn't. Sleeping the day away wouldn't help. He was responsible now, and regardless of what he wanted, he needed to go see Blake and let him know what had gone down.

He pulled up to the library. His brother took one look at him and his eyebrows pinched together in worry. He could always read Trevor like a book. Trevor was the same way with Blake. It wasn't until his eyes scanned down Trevor's body and landed on his hand that he pulled his hard hat off and walked Trevor's way.

"What happened to you?" he pointed to Trevor's hand.

"I cut it. It's not a big deal. It's going to be a good job for us. He wants some pretty heavy remodeling done. It'll keep us busy for a few months. I told him I'd sit down with you and we'd get him some more information within the next couple days."

"Great. Sounds good. It went well, then?"

"Yeah," Trevor lied. He hated doing it but he didn't have it in him to go there with Blake right now.

"What about the hand? How long are you out? That's going to factor in. Plus, it'll take us a little longer to finish here—"

"It'll be fine. I'll be fine," Trevor lied again. His hand would hurt like a bitch but he would deal with it. He would work. "It's not that bad. I'm going to have to take today off, though."

“Yeah, sure. Of course.” Blake’s eyes stared into Trevor’s. He always did that when he wanted to try and figure out what Trevor was thinking or if he was telling the truth. The bastard knew him too well. Trevor diverted his eyes, and felt like an ass while doing it.

“I’m going to head out. You guys will be okay today?”

“Yep. We got this. Go home and get some rest,” Blake replied. Trevor made it all the way to his truck before Blake called out to him. “Trev?”

The question was there without his brother having asked it. He let out a heavy breath and turned. “We’re all good, little brother. I denied the prescription and wouldn’t take anything at the hospital, either.”

“I’m sorry.” Blake hated to ask, Trevor knew that. It didn’t make it any easier to swallow. It was bullshit that he *had* to ask, but that was no one’s fault except Trevor’s.

“I know. See you at home tonight.” Trevor climbed into his truck and drove away.

***

Simon held the scalpel in his hand. Tried to tighten his hold on it the way he should. Not too tightly, but with the right amount of pressure so he could keep it steady and cut with a gentle, skilled hand.

His hand tingled. It fucking shook and he couldn’t stop it. And it hurt. His fingers didn’t want to work the way they should to hold onto the tool he previously wielded so well. Not without pain darting through his hand and wrist.

“Fuck!” Simon threw the instrument on the table. He was pissed at himself for getting hurt. For not healing the way he should, or realizing the pressure being put on his nerves right after the injury. At the construction worker for making such a stupid, fucking mistake.

How good could his skill level be if he couldn't even walk through a house without ripping his hand open?

It was his fault Simon had to step foot in that hospital today. To smell the antiseptics, instead of just remembering them. For taking him to the place he had no business being at because he couldn't do what he wanted there.

Suddenly he felt like he'd taken the bat to his hand just recently, the wounds and the news of mononeuropathy damage still fresh in his ears.

The phone rang, and without looking at it, Simon knew who it was. He didn't feel like talking to her, but he also knew Heather. If he didn't answer, she wouldn't stop calling. She may even jump in her car and make the drive from San Francisco to Rockford Falls. Maybe he needed that. Maybe he needed to see her.

He'd loved Heather one way or another for many years. If anyone could pull him out of his funk, it would be her. But she couldn't. She'd already tried.

"Hey you," she said when Simon picked up, before he even had the chance to say hello.

"Hello."

"What are you doing?" Heather asked.

"Throwing a temper tantrum."

She chuckled. "No surprise there. How'd it go today? I think you'll feel better once work on the house starts."

No, he wanted to tell her. He would feel better if his fucking hand worked right.

"It was a disaster. The man cut his hand open and I had to drive him to the hospital to get it stitched up."

"Oh…" was all Heather said. She knew he avoided hospitals like the plague.

"Exactly."

She obviously decided it was a good idea to change the subject because she asked, "Alan and I wanted to see if you had plans this weekend."

She knew he didn't.

"We thought you might want to come and meet us for dinner." Alan was her boyfriend, and one of Simon's ex-colleagues. She'd started dating him a little over two months after Simon's accident—accident, ha; the day someone *accidentally* broke into his house and *accidentally* took a bat to his hand—and they'd been together ever since.

Simon was happy for her. As much as he loved her, he'd never been able to give her what she needed. Surgery had been his mistress. It was his first and only love.

"No, thanks. I appreciate the offer."

"Hey…you can talk to me, Simon. I know you never did before, but I always thought that was because you were too busy for words."

Really, it was just that he sucked at them. He did better with unconscious people than he did everyone else. "I'm fine, Heather. Tell

Alan I said hello."

Right after he ended the call, Simon made another one.

CHAPTER FOUR

It was Saturday, but Trevor couldn't sleep past seven. If he was being honest, he'd admit he missed sleeping half the day away and being up until all hours of the night. He felt sixty instead of twenty-five now. He rarely stayed up past ten, and he was up by seven every weekend, and earlier for work during the week.

Being idle was hard on him now. When he sat around, he thought. When he thought, he remembered. When he remembered, he craved.

"Want to go on a jog with me?" Trevor wore sweats and a T-shirt, the little metal chip in his pocket that he always kept with him. Evidence of his sobriety.

Blake sat at the kitchen table in his boxers, nursing a cup of coffee. "It's seven."

"No shit, Sherlock. Get your lazy ass dressed and come run with me." Trevor picked up a hand towel from the counter and threw it at Blake.

"Are you sure it's a good idea to run with your hand?"

Trevor grinned at him. "Don't usually run with my hand."

Blake rolled his eyes.

"Come on, little brother. Let's go. I'll beat your ass in a run and then we'll come home and talk about that job."

His brother's eyes darted away at that, and Trevor knew. He fucking *knew* what that meant. "He called you, didn't he? He called and said we didn't get the job."

"Last night."

"Fuck." Trevor dropped his head backward and looked at the ceiling. *Running. He loved running now. Mom, Blake, Rock Solid...* though maybe Rock Solid wasn't something he would have to enjoy or be thankful for soon. Not if they weren't working enough.

"It takes time to get a business off the ground, Trev."

"No shit," he replied. It pissed him off when his brother pretended to know better than Trevor did. As though Trevor was stupid just because he'd been an addict like their dad.

"It happens. It wasn't your fault. We can't get them all."

He groaned. "Please don't try and make me feel better." It only made him feel like more of a fuck up, though he knew that wasn't what Blake wanted to do.

"Excuse me for trying to help." Blake pushed to his feet.

"It doesn't. It makes me feel like shit."

"Fuck you, Trev. You can be a real asshole, you know that?"

He did know it. He also knew he wasn't going to give up this job without a fight. Things changed. He didn't walk away from his problems. Not anymore.

Without replying to Blake, he grabbed his truck keys from the counter and pushed past his brother. That easily, Blake knew exactly what Trevor had planned.

"Don't do this, Trev. You're just going to make things worse."

Not this time. His days of making things worse were in the past.

***

Simon sat on the edge of his bed when the pounding on his front door started. His heart jumped, thinking something was wrong, until he made his way to the window to see Trevor standing on his porch.

Bang, bang, bang.

The fist of his good hand came down on the door again. His good hand. He had one good and one bad, just the way Simon did, only Trevor's would heal completely, and surgery hadn't done the job for Simon's.

But then he realized what was going on here. Who the hell did this kid think he was, banging on Simon's door like that? Simon made his way into the living room and jerked the door open. "What the hell are you doing?"

"Asking you to reconsider," Trevor said through pursed lips.

"Asking me to reconsider? You thought by coming to my home at seven thirty on a Saturday morning, and banging on my door, you'd get me to consider hiring your company? Think again, kid."

Trevor pushed his hand through his dark hair, and winced. Simon knew how sore it had to be if he wasn't taking anything for it. "I'm not a kid."

No, Simon guessed he wasn't. He probably had ten years on Trevor, but he wasn't a kid. "You're acting like one. This is business. I made the best business decision for myself. It happens. Get used to it."

Simon tried to close the door but Trevor's left hand shot out and stopped it. He opened his mouth to tell the guy to back the hell off when Trevor spoke. "Is it because you realized I'm in recovery? I've been clean for over a year. No slip-ups. My past isn't pretty but I'm working on changing that. It isn't going to affect the job."

The pain in Trevor's voice radiated off him, slamming into Simon. He got that kind of pain. He felt it. And it took balls for Trevor to admit his past to Simon.

"It's not that."

Trevor sighed. "I can promise you we'll do a good job. I'll drive you around and show you jobs we've done. Hell, I'll do some work for you outside of the remodel, no charge, just so you can see my work ethic."

"Your hand—"

"Please," Trevor cut him off. "I have no right to ask you this. I have no right to be here. I get it. But I'm here asking you anyway. We'll do a damn good job for you. I'll make sure of it. I'm trying to get my shit together, and I know that's not your problem. My past, my problem. But I'm also trying not to take other people down with me. If I keep them from getting work, that's what I'm doing. I'm trying to move on. My past isn't who I am." He shrugged as though he had nothing else in him to give. The darkness in his eyes said he hated what he already gave. Hated asking, and giving Simon that piece of him.

Simon got that too.

"Who are you?" Simon found himself asking. It was a strange question. He didn't know where in the hell it had come from, but the man said his past wasn't who he was. Simon suddenly wanted to know who he thought he'd become.

"That's what I'm trying to figure out," he replied. Trevor's words bounced around in his head. They mirrored Simon.

He knew all too well. He used to be Dr. Simon Malone, cardio-thoracic surgeon, but now he was a surgeon with a fucked up hand. A surgeon who couldn't perform surgery, which meant he wasn't a surgeon at all.

Simon took the man in. He was lost, in the same way Simon was.

Trevor looked as though he was ready to go work out, in sweats and running shoes. It's what Simon had been ready to go do himself.

He had two choices here. He could tell Trevor to fuck off…or he could give him a chance. The truth was, there was something about him that Simon connected with. He had balls. Coming over here had been a stupid thing for Trevor to do, but he hadn't let that hold him back. He'd done what he believed he had to, no matter how hard it was. Simon could respect that. Everything he'd done yesterday had shown how gutsy he was, too, and how strong. No one in that emergency room would have known Trevor wasn't supposed to take the medication, if he'd accepted it. But he hadn't.

Simon stepped out of the house and closed the door behind him. He paused. "Go for a run with me."

Trevor nodded, and then the two of them jogged down his stairs and headed for the road.

CHAPTER FIVE

Trevor's hand ached. Pain shot through it each time one of his feet hit the ground, the vibration echoing up through his body. Still, he kept going. It felt good to run. He started as soon as he'd gotten clean and he hadn't stopped ever since.

He liked when his lungs hurt. When he gasped for cleansing breath, because he hadn't felt clean when he was using. It took getting clean for him to realize it.

Simon ran beside him. Their arms brushed up against one another's every once in a while. Each time it did, Trevor couldn't stop wondering what they were doing out here. They hadn't gotten along very well yesterday. Add in Trevor's irresponsible behavior from today, and he would fully understand why Simon wouldn't want to hire them, or want Trevor on his property again.

Yet, here they were, running the twisting, forested road together.

"So, you're a doctor." Trevor concentrated on breathing, and the sound of their feet slamming down on the ground. The silence was killing him. He had to say something.

"Yes."

"You said something about working in San Francisco, but you live out here."

Plop, plop, plop, plop, their footsteps blended together as they beat on the ground.

"I'm retired."

Obviously, Simon wasn't much of a talker. "Aren't you a little young for that?"

He turned his head, his left eyebrow going up. "I'm older than you."

"Yeah, but I'm not retired."

Simon's black hair lay plastered with sweat against his head. He was older than Trevor, but he couldn't be *too* much older. He had no wrinkles around his eyes, or gray in his hair. He was cute. Probably as straight as they came, but sexy.

Simon turned away. "Let's head back." They made a quick turn and then continued their jog back toward Simon's house. Obviously, he didn't plan on giving Trevor an answer, and that annoyed him. He wasn't sure why he wanted one so damned much.

"I was attacked. A home invasion. Swelling and pressure on the wrong nerves screwed up my career. Can't very well perform surgery if you can't grip a scalpel or control the pain in your hand." He didn't look at Trevor, but he didn't have to for Trevor to hear the anger, and pain, in his voice.

It made the air around them tight, stifling.

Simon surprised him by adding, "It's all I ever wanted to do."

“Shit, man. I’m sorry.” And he was. He couldn’t imagine losing something like that. He’d been pretty lucky in his life. He’d done nothing but fuck up, yet he still had family who loved him. People who were willing to put themselves on the line by starting a business with him. Maybe Simon had that, too, but he’d obviously lost a part of himself as well.

Trevor had too. Not a good part of himself, but he’d lost a part all the same. “I started drinking heavily when I was sixteen. Moved on to pills by eighteen. Harder drugs after that. I didn’t go to college, or have a career before now. I didn’t have goals, but I had partying. I thought I liked my life at the time. I thought that was who I was. It’s a good thing…losing that. I wouldn’t have it any other way, but it was still a loss. I’m twenty-five now, and it’s hard to figure out who you are when the one thing you think defines you is gone.”

He felt Simon’s arm brush against his again, but this time…he could have sworn it lingered.

“Thank you,” was all Simon said. They ran back to his house in the first comfortable silence they’d had between them.

***

Since the attack, Simon hadn’t really spoken to anyone. Not seriously. Heather tried to talk to him about it, but it had been impossible to talk to his ex-wife, and she was all Simon had. She’d always been the only person in his life. But he still couldn’t open up to her, couldn’t find the words. He pretended none of it mattered.

That was nothing new. He was a good doctor for a lot of reasons. One of them being that while he felt empathy and cared for people, he was good at turning off his emotions when he needed to. He could close himself off and make things not bother him, or at least he found a way not to show it.

It's what he'd done since realizing the first surgery hadn't been a success. He pretended to accept it and move on, even though he didn't. He couldn't.

What he'd just told Trevor was nothing. Not really. Yet, it felt like something. It felt like he'd shared more on that jog with Trevor than he had with anyone else since he lost his ability to perform surgery.

Mostly because he felt the same way Trevor did. When he thanked Trevor, he'd admitted as much. In that sense, he spoke to Trevor.

The why of it he still wasn't totally sold on. Probably because they were experiencing the same thing in a strange, backward way.

It was that knowledge that made him stop when they reached the porch and say, "Do you want to come in for a drink?" When Trevor's eyes went wide, Simon realized how it sounded. "Coffee, water, orange juice or tea, you smartass."

"Hey, I didn't say anything."

"You didn't have to."

He smiled. "Yeah, sure. Water sounds good."

Simon led Trevor inside. It wasn't as though he had very far to go. This was the smallest house he'd lived in since his dorm in college. "Have a seat." He nodded at the table. "Bottled or glass? It's from the filter in the fridge, so it's clean."

"Ummm…" Trevor sat down and eyed him. "Honestly? I can't tell the difference. Whatever's easier, man."

Simon grabbed two bottles of water from the fridge and tossed one to Trevor. He watched as the man twisted the lid off. Watched his throat muscles work as he swallowed it all down without a break. He had plump lips for a man. Not overly so, but they gave Trevor a unique look.

Simon shifted uncomfortably before leaning against the counter in the kitchen. "You can't work for a couple weeks."

Trevor looked down and picked at the paper on his empty water bottle. "That's not your problem. It's mine. I know what I can handle. I'll be okay. Even if I wasn't here working, that doesn't mean the other guys couldn't be." He looked up. "They're hard workers. They'll be able to do exactly what you need. They shouldn't have my shit held against them."

Simon let out a deep breath, trying to figure out why he felt he needed to do this so badly. It didn't make sense. "I already said it had nothing to do with your past. I honestly wasn't sure if you were the right person for the job. Add that in with the fact that I was being an asshole because of my issues and there you have my decision."

"Jason has an eye like no one I've ever seen. He can look at a building or a house and see things I'd never see. He can tell if something's going to work or not before anyone else can. Andrea's brickwork is incredible. Blake is the smartest person I know. JT's been doing this almost as long as I've been alive. We're the right people for the job."

Simon opened his water bottle and took a few drinks. It was a way to stall. To try and figure out what in the hell he was doing. On the one hand, it wasn't a big deal. He was considering hiring someone to remodel his house. It had been the plan all along. On the other hand, it was more than that. He was considering hiring someone who he originally wasn't sure would do a good job. Someone he just spent an hour going on a jog with, where Simon admitted he wasn't sure who he was without being a heart surgeon.

Someone he thought might get him in a strange, confusing way.

It was the doctor in him who replied, though. "You have the job if you can wait until your hand heals."

That was a lie. He hadn't answered as a doctor. He'd answered as the man who just saw somewhat of a kindred spirit in another man. It hadn't escaped Simon's attention that Trevor talked about what everyone could bring to the table except himself.

"We didn't write up an estimate for you or anything. I only asked for a fair chance. Let me get some paperwork put together for you. I'll bring it by tomorrow. If you like what you see then, we have a deal."

Simon nodded his head, thankful when Trevor stood up to leave.

CHAPTER SIX

Trevor was fully aware that he was avoiding his brother by not going straight home. It probably hadn't been the smartest idea for the two of them to be roommates and to run a business together, but he figured Blake had made the suggestion as a way to keep an eye on him.

Honestly, Trevor didn't think that was such a bad thing. Most days he was fine, but like anyone in recovery, he had his hard times. And even though sometimes things were a struggle between himself and Blake, the man was his twin. His other half. No one would ever understand Trevor the way Blake would.

Still, he wasn't in the mood for questions about Simon or to hear Blake tell him how irresponsible it was for him to go, regardless of the fact that he'd gotten them a second chance.

So, instead of going home or trying to find something else to do (what did an ex-alcoholic and drug addict do for fun? He wasn't even sure), Trevor pulled over and looked up the schedule of meetings on his phone.

He had his sponsor, and he typically went to meetings once a week at Cedarhill Recovery, but they had meetings a few other places in town as well. Trevor had been to them all. It couldn't hurt.

It didn't take him long to get over to Rockford Bridge for their NA meeting. His skin felt itchy and tight, as it always did when he walked inside. Even after all this time, he couldn't believe he had to be here or that things had gotten so bad, so out of hand, that he'd spent months in inpatient to get clean. That he'd gotten so drunk and high that he got in a car with a friend behind the wheel who was even more wasted than he was.

It was a blessing they hadn't hurt or killed anyone else that day. Greg hadn't been so lucky. After he and Trevor separated, Greg had gone right over the steering wheel and out the window. Trevor had ditched him and lay in the middle of nowhere in his own vomit while his friend (was he even a friend?) died.

Trevor rubbed his eyes with the heels of his hands, trying to keep his mind from going back to the car that night.

He reminded himself that it was a good, responsible thing that he came to a meeting today. He needed to keep making decisions like that.

After Trevor climbed out of his truck, he made his way inside the building. The meeting had started about five minutes ago, so Trevor quietly slipped his way in and found a chair at the back of the room. He held his sobriety token as he listened. There was a woman with graying hair standing at the front. She talked about forgiveness, and trying to find it in herself after everything she'd done.

Trevor could understand that. He lived in constant regret of all the things he'd done while trying to make up for them. How did you make up for the past? He wasn't sure he could, but not trying wasn't an option, either.

He'd been so lucky in his life. He was born with a best friend who would do anything for him, to a mother who loved her sons unconditionally. He never had to worry about acceptance from her. Neither Dixon boy had. His father had been the only black mark on their lives—an alcoholic who functioned much better than Trevor had in the fact that he went to work every day and no one outside of their family knew. It was a secret that he drank half the night, every night. That he would call them all names, and curse them out when he did.

He never hit them, but the verbal abuse had been enough.

How in the hell Trevor managed to lose himself down the same bottle, he'd never know.

"I've realized it's killing me, the looking back, the trying to make excuses for everything I did, or trying to make amends for it now," the woman continued.

Yeah, Trevor got that. He'd done it all—been bailed out of jail, stolen, broken hearts. It weighed on his mind every second of every day. He couldn't stop focusing on the *why* of it all, and he would never stop trying to make up for it.

***

Simon spent the day doing a whole lot of nothing. It was a struggle getting used to that. When he'd become a surgeon, he was important for the first time in his life. He was doing something that mattered. Nothing he'd done mattered before that. Not to himself, and not enough to get his father's attention.

And now he did nothing.

Well, that wasn't completely true. He always had his laptop close. There were endless medical articles for him to read, some he'd written himself.

But today he'd spent most of his time thinking about his morning with Trevor.

Simon didn't do things like that. He didn't ask people to jog with him. He typically didn't change his mind, either. If he decided something, that was it. If he didn't think someone was cut out for a job, he didn't hire them.

Hell, when he first moved here the plumbing had been screwed up. He hired a man, who showed up forty-five minutes late, and Simon met him at the door and let him know he'd hired someone else. The replacement plumber wouldn't come until two hours after he sent the first away, but those two hours weren't because the man just ran late without calling. Those kinds of things bothered Simon.

Yet unlike the plumber, he'd given Trevor a second chance, and he wasn't sure what to think about that. He'd spent an hour on a pros and cons list of hiring Rock Solid, if that said anything for his confusion. Cons won, yet he wasn't sure it mattered.

He'd seen a hidden piece of himself in Trevor. A part that felt unsure, was angry, that wanted something they didn't have.

Somehow, it had made him feel a little less alone.

As much as he hated that, hated feeling insecure about himself in any way, or feeling an unexplainable connection to a man he didn't know, Simon couldn't deny that he felt it. Couldn't deny that it intrigued him.

It felt like giving Trevor another shot was the right thing to do. Or maybe he just wanted it to be, because of that fucking intrigue. Simon wasn't sure he often did the right thing, so this was probably more for him in whatever way, than it was for Trevor.

He shook his head. He needed to stop overthinking everything, yet that's who he was. It always had been.

Simon moved to his bed. He could take a nap. That would make his brain shut down. It wasn't as though he had anything else to do.

But it didn't work. It rarely did.

He thought about the last heart he'd held in his hand. How many people could say they'd held someone's heart in their hand? Not in the way you did when you loved someone, but an actual beating heart.

"I decided I'm doing the surgery."

His colleague's eyes widened. "It'll happen without you, Dr. Malone. You don't have to do it. Over at county hospital—"

"They're not as good as I am and you know it." Simon smiled. He loved being that good. He knew he was.

"Yes, but they also will get paid for it in a way that you won't. There's no insurance."

The way his fellow surgeon spoke, almost made Simon feel stupid, like an amateur, but then...this is what he'd gotten into surgery for, wasn't it? To save lives. To matter. This mattered. What he did mattered.

"You're not the one who should be doing this and you know it." She shrugged as though they weren't talking about a person.

"I'm the only one who should be doing it." Because he could save her. Because saving people was all that mattered. Because Simon performed miracles.

A week later as he'd held her heart in his hand, her chest open in front of him, the beep and comforting lull of machines around him, he'd known he made the right decision, pro bono or not.

He might be a surly bastard sometimes. He might not know how to love people. He might not have ever had many people who'd loved him in his life, but he had this.

Simon's eyes jerked open, nausea rolling through his gut.

He used to have it.

CHAPTER SEVEN

When Trevor woke up Sunday morning for his run, Blake wasn't up yet. He hadn't been home when Trevor got in the night before, either. He felt a little sting of jealousy that his brother had probably gone out, had a few drinks with friends, maybe went home with someone and had sex.

Jesus, he missed sex. He hadn't had it in over a year.

Blake could do those things, though; Trevor couldn't. Well, the sex he could, but it was different being sober. Where do you pick someone up when you can't go to a bar or a club? He wasn't into dating apps. Meeting up for anonymous sex wasn't his thing.

He considered calling Simon. Maybe the man would want to go on another run with him? It never hurt to have someone there to keep you motivated, but in the end, he decided against it. The first time they met, Simon looked down his nose at Trevor. The fact that they'd gone on a run together yesterday, and Simon agreed to give them a chance, didn't change anything. There was no reason to try to pretend they were all buddy-buddy.

As it always did, running cleared Trevor's head. By the time he stumbled back into the small house he shared with his brother, sweaty and out of breath, Blake was home.

"Hey, big brother." Blake smiled, guilt clouding his eyes.

"Hey, little brother. You know, you don't have to stay gone all night." It was pretty shitty that Blake thought he couldn't have a couple beers with friends and then come home out of fear of being a temptation to Trevor. His gut twisted at that, the thought that he didn't think Trevor was strong enough to handle it.

"Shit," Blake mumbled and then ran a hand through his hair the same way Trevor did. "We were watching the race. It was only a couple of beers."

"You could have had more, you know. My shit isn't your problem. We all know you have your head too put together to follow down my path." That truth hurt, but it was, in fact, a truth.

"It's an asshole thing to do…coming home after drinking. Feels that way, at least, but now I'm feeling like just as big an asshole for not coming home. I don't…" Blake shook his head.

Yeah. Trevor didn't know how to do this, either, so he changed the subject. "Where'd you stay?"

"Jason's."

Trevor didn't try to hold back his grin. "You two getting back together? It's only a matter of time." Imagine their mom's surprise to find out not one, but both of her sons were gay. She didn't flinch when she found out. It never bothered her. She just smiled and said, "It makes sense that it's both of you. Neither of you ever wanted to do anything without the other. Just don't let any boys come between you."

Then they'd all laughed and that was that.

And Trevor had gone on to do a shit ton of things without his brother, things he was glad Blake never participated in.

"We're not getting back together. We're not sleeping with each other, either. We're friends. Trying to make it more would be a mistake. We both know that." He crossed his arms and leaned against the back of the couch.

"Okay." Trevor nodded. "Then get your ass home instead of staying with him. If you're not getting your dick sucked out of the deal, you should at least get to stay in your own bed. No matter what, okay?" He wanted to make sure his brother got that. This was Blake's home. Blake's life. He shouldn't have to censor it for Trevor. "I can handle it."

"Yeah…yeah, sure." He walked over and playfully shoved Trevor, and Trevor knew that despite the okay, he wouldn't listen. "So where the hell did you go when you stormed out of here yesterday? I'm not going to have to kick your ass, am I?"

Trevor smiled. "You can kiss my ass is what you can do. I got us a second chance. Come on." He pointed to the kitchen table. "We have work to do, like getting a proposal written up for Simon."

The pride in Blake's face made some of the weight lift off Trevor's shoulders.

***

It was close to four when there was a knock on Simon's door. He minimized the screen on his computer, not as though anything he'd been searching would do him any good anyway. Obsessively looking up information on his hand wouldn't change anything. Surgery was usually a good option…but for Simon it hadn't worked. Part of him accepted that, but the compulsion to look was always there.

Frustration burned at his insides. He'd expected Trevor to come before this. If the man wanted the job that badly, a person would assume he'd come first thing. It's what Simon would have done.

He opened the door. "Found the time to make it, did you?"

Trevor's dark brows pulled together. "Did I miss something? I said I would come today and I did. It's only three fifty. We wanted to be as thorough as possible."

Which made perfect sense, and Simon was well aware he was being an asshole. "You're right. I apologize. It's been a long day." *A long day of doing nothing.* He still wasn't used to it. Simon had always worked and worked hard: college, medical school, residency, getting board certified for cardiology, and general surgery. He'd been at the top of his class, yearning for more knowledge every step of the way. He worked overtime and studied his craft, always trying to learn more. Wanting to perform miracles. It had been his life. Heather could attest to that. And now he had nothing to do with his time, and that was killing him.

"Come in." He stepped out of Trevor's way. Trevor lingered for a second before coming in. He crossed the small living room and went for the table, folders and papers in his hands.

"It's only been a day. Take that into consideration. Anything can be changed. We drew up a few ideas for you, wrote up what you told us and got some prices together. My co-owner had to go off my notes. Hurt like a bitch to try and write. I think you'll find we're comparable to anyone around here. Probably a little less."

"Okay," Simon replied. It felt like a ridiculous answer, though he wasn't sure why. "Have a seat."

Trevor pulled out a chair and sat. He began picking papers out of folders and spreading them out on the tabletop. His hands were beaten and rough. There was sun damage, which Simon almost brought up. He should take care of his skin. He should take care of his hands.

Simon sat beside him. They were different men with different jobs. They used their hands in different ways. Besides the surgery scar, there was nothing cosmetically wrong with Simon's. No callouses or wear and tear, yet his were broken for what he needed to do. After a couple weeks, Trevor's would be fine. The bandage would be gone and he would make a full recovery.

They spent the next hour going over the proposal. There were a few changes that Simon wanted, primarily to his office and library area. It's where he would write his book. What the hell else did he have to do with his time other than that?

He had to admit, though, that what Trevor had put together was pretty spot on. He obviously knew what he was doing. Many things he'd brought up Simon hadn't considered, or didn't know about.

He leaned back in his chair. "It's yours if you want it, but my stipulation from yesterday stands. Not until your hand is healed. And I want you to oversee it." The last part was an unexpected addition but one Simon felt secure in.

Lines formed around Trevor's eyes. The blue in them seemed to swirl, trying to focus as though they couldn't, and then his dark brows pulled together again. "Blake usually—"

"Good for Blake. You're the one I've spoken to. You're the one I want."

Trevor's eyes sparked, almost looked ablaze with…Simon wasn't sure what. He recovered quickly and said, "You're a bossy son-of-a-bitch, aren't you?"

It probably wasn't the best thing to say to a prospective employer. No one Simon knew would have spoken to him in such a manner, but it didn't bother him that Trevor did. He chuckled. Hell, maybe he even liked that Trevor did.

"Shit. I'm sorry. I—" Trevor started.

"It's okay."

"There's a reason Blake usually does the talking." Trevor's lips tightened slightly when he said that. Not in anger, Simon didn't think.

"Eh. You keep people on their toes." He would keep Simon that way. He word-vomited sometimes like no one Simon ever knew.

Trevor was silent for a moment. Simon could practically see the wheels turning in his head. "Thank you. I appreciate it. You won't regret it."

Somehow, Simon didn't think he would.

The silence in the room was interrupted when Trevor's stomach growled. They were still sitting close; other chairs were at the table but they still sat next to each other despite the fact that they weren't looking at paperwork anymore.

And Simon didn't want to move. He wasn't the type of man who enjoyed being overly close to people. He didn't understand all the touching and hugging people often participated in, but in this moment, being close to Trevor didn't bother him. "I'd offer you something to eat but I'm not sure I have anything."

Trevor scooted his chair back. "Supercross is on tonight. If you're just going to be hanging around here, we can order a pizza and watch it."

Simon laughed. He'd catch hell for this one. "That would work if I had a television."

Trevor's eyes went wide. "How in the hell do you not have a TV? You're a thirty-year-old guy and you don't have a TV? What's wrong with you, man?" He laughed.

"Thirty-seven, and no, I don't." This is where he should thank Trevor, let the guy pack up his stuff and go…but the truth was, the thought of sitting in this house another minute made Simon's skin crawl. He needed out. Needed to *do* something. "Let's go grab a burger or something and we can watch it."

"Yeah, sounds good." Trevor's smile slowly started to slip off his face. He let out a deep breath and said, "Where?"

He couldn't go to a bar, and that apparently bothered him. Not because he wanted to drink so badly, Simon didn't think, but just because he *couldn't*, and he figured Simon would want to.

"You've lived here longer than me. Where's a good place to go? You mentioned pizza. Most pizza joints have a few televisions going."

There was another thank you in Trevor's eyes. "Yeah, okay. Come on. I'll drive."

CHAPTER EIGHT

"I know I keep harping on this, but I can't get over the fact that you don't have a TV. That doesn't even compute to me." Trevor took a drink of his iced tea and then leaned back in his seat. It wasn't that he sat around watching hours of reality shows and sitcoms every night, but who didn't have a TV? There were sports out there. Didn't Simon know that?

"Because while you were watching sports on TV, I was studying. You look like you would have been the jock in high school, and I was the nerd. We wouldn't have been friends." Simon paused. Trevor was about to tell him that he might have been a jock but he was even more of a troublemaker when Simon continued. "Actually, we wouldn't have been friends because while I was in high school and college, you were in elementary school." He shook his head. His neatly trimmed dark hair didn't move. Everything was neat about Simon. His clothes always looked neat. The man didn't even have a day's growth of stubble on his face. Nothing but his square jaw, that he tightened often. His round, inquisitive eyes that almost looked gray, and a sexy mouth. Simon definitely turned him on. It had been a long time for Trevor.

"Well then, I guess it's a good thing we didn't meet until now," Trevor said, and he meant it. He enjoyed Simon's company more than he thought he would. Then, Trevor grinned, a thought jumping into his head. "Old man," he teased, only to have Simon's eyes narrow on him.

"Christ, don't remind me." He sounded more serious than Trevor thought he would.

"I'm giving you shit. Thirty-seven isn't old. You're only as old as you feel."

Which was kind of shitty for Trevor because most days, he felt like he'd lived enough life to be eighty.

"That's not helping, because I sure as hell feel a lot older than thirty-seven."

Trevor smiled, and took another drink of his tea.

"Is that funny? The fact that I'm old?" There was more of a playful tone to Simon's voice now.

"No, I just thought it was a coincidence because I was thinking the same thing. I feel three times as old as I am."

There was a silence then between them. Trevor couldn't help but wonder if Simon was thinking how they had a few things in common. They seemed to feel the same about a lot. Somehow he knew Simon was thinking along the same lines. And maybe that made it a good thing that Trevor was pretty sure Simon was straight. Sex would complicate things, and right now, maybe he needed a friend more than sex.

"Your taste in pizza is questionable." Simon set his slice of pepperoni down. Trevor agreed with him.

"I haven't been here since before I was clean. It didn't used to taste this bad, I don't think." Because it was pretty fucking awful. A memory popped into Trevor's head. "Or maybe I just have shit taste. When I was a kid, I used to think I was a good cook. Every Mother's Day and on Mom's birthday I used to 'treat' her to breakfast in bed." He shook his head and chuckled. "It was shitty. How badly can you fuck up breakfast? But I did it. Burnt toast and under-cooked eggs. She always ate it, though, and I kept making it." He'd forgotten about that. "I haven't thought of that in years."

Being drunk or high did that to a guy, he guessed.

"She loves you, so to her it was a treat." Simon leaned his elbows on the table. "I'm a horrible cook too, but I never took the time to try to make food for anyone I cared about. Too busy studying." He raised his eyebrows. "Books were always my thing."

They had never been Trevor's. "Maybe if they'd been mine, I wouldn't have gotten myself in all the shit I did." He would do anything to go back, to find a way to change it all. But he couldn't. Life didn't work that way.

***

Their conversation took a slightly somber tone, though Simon wasn't really sure why. Still, he didn't want to stop talking. He enjoyed getting to know Trevor. Hell, he couldn't remember the last time he'd really gotten to know anyone. "You said 'before.' Before what?" he asked. Maybe he shouldn't have, because the blue in Trevor's eyes stormed over.

"Before everything. Mostly, before I left for rehab, though… The race is over." Trevor nodded toward the television. They hadn't really watched any of it. They'd sat here and talked for hours. That had to be some kind of record for Simon. He wasn't much of a talker.

"I guess it is." Trevor didn't reply, and Simon didn't say anything, either. He weighed his thoughts before speaking. Most of the time, he was pretty good at that. This could be a huge mistake. It probably was. He wasn't great at being friends. Still, he asked. "What are you doing tomorrow morning?" Before Trevor could answer, Simon's phone buzzed.

"Go ahead." Trevor crossed his arms and waited.

Simon looked at the screen on his cell. "It's Heather, my ex. I can call her back later."

Trevor flinched at that, though Simon wasn't sure why. The pause stretched on for another minute or so before Trevor spoke. "If I had an ex call me right now…actually, I've never had a long term relationship, but if someone I'd been with called me, it would be a man. I'm not sure if that matters as far as this friendship goes."

Simon's answer was automatic, "It doesn't." Why the hell would it? What he couldn't stop focusing on was Trevor's use of the word friendship. When was the last time he'd really made friends with anyone? Sure he had work colleagues, and he had Heather. It wasn't as though he was a hermit or anything, but friends had never really been high on his priority list before. Now, he really didn't have a priority list.

"Then nope, I don't have plans tomorrow morning. Can't work. I cut my hand on a nail in some guy's house. He really should get that fixed."

Simon laughed. “Sounds to me like you need to watch where you’re going.”

“Figures. It’s always my fault. You’d think I’d be used to it by now.” Trevor winked.

“If you’re up for it, I’m going for a jog in the morning. You’re welcome to join me if you want.” Simon actually wanted him to. It was the first time besides wanting his hand to work that Simon remembered wanting anything in a long time.

CHAPTER NINE

They saw each other every day for the next two weeks. Some days it was only for their morning jog. Others they would grab a bite to eat, walk up to Simon's main house to talk about the remodel, meet and watch a game or Supercross at the shitty pizza joint. Trevor used to love riding dirt bikes, though he hadn't done it in years. Watching Supercross reminded him of his old passion.

The men had become good friends. Trevor's mind was always going with crap, but it somehow helped when he hung out with Simon. It gave him something else to focus on. He noticed that helped, having things to keep his attention. It made the desire to find something to drink or take a lot weaker.

It was the day before Trevor got his stitches out. They'd just finished their morning run when Simon told him, "You'll be proud of me. I'm going out to buy a television today."

Trevor looked at him over the hood of his truck. They were both sweaty and shirtless, Simon breathing a little heavier then Trevor. Forcing his eyes to veer away, Trevor leaned on his truck. The man was sexy, a light dusting of dark hair on his chest. Abdominal muscles with enough definition to show, but it also didn't look like he spent hours in the gym, which was fine with Trevor. He wasn't really into the overly-muscled man. He liked being broader than the men he was with. Not that he was a gym-rat himself, but his work helped with that. Also, it wasn't as if he would be with Simon, sexy or not.

His whole body looked clean, if that made sense. No scars, he didn't have tattoos like the ones Trevor had on his right arm. Simon reminded him of something new when Trevor himself felt old and used.

The truth was, he was much more attracted to Simon than he should be. If things were different, Trevor would take more time to admire him. But even if Simon was gay, he had no business going there. Not just because they would be remodeling Simon's home. Hell, not even because getting involved with someone wasn't the best idea until he made sure he had his head together a little more. The main reason was he just didn't want to lose him as a friend. He enjoyed spending time with Simon too much. Blake and Jason made a friendship work outside of sex and dating, but considering Trevor had never really done the dating thing, just the sex thing, he didn't want to take the chance.

TV. That's what they were talking about. He had to get his head back in the game. "Yeah? It's about time. I don't have anything going on until my meeting tonight. If you want, I'll ride with you." Because Simon couldn't pick out a TV on his own. Yeah, right.

Simon nodded. "That sounds good. I'm going to shower and eat some lunch. Does one work for you?"

"Sure. I'll be here at one." Trevor walked to the door of his truck and opened it. He winked at Simon. "See ya then, Dr. Malone." It was a reflex really, a joke, but every one of Simon's features hardened. He looked like the man Trevor met the first day, instead of the guy he'd become friends with. "Hey, sorry. I didn't mean…" Did Simon think Trevor was hitting on him because of the wink, or was it the doctor thing?

"It's okay. I'll see you at one." Simon turned away without another word. He made it halfway to his door before Trevor called out to him.

"Hey!"

Simon stopped. Waited and then turned. A heavy breath fell from Trevor's lungs when he did. "I'm an asshole." Though he still wasn't sure why.

Simon shook his head. "No, you're not. I'll see you soon." He walked into his house, his back muscles flexing as he did.

"Fuck." He had no idea what that was about. Trevor sighed, got into his truck and drove away.

***

"You see, TVs come in all different sizes nowadays. They even have smart TVs, and TVs you can use to watch the internet. We'll get into a discussion on the internet another day. I don't want to overwhelm you with modern technology." Trevor nudged Simon's arm with his own as they walked through the electronics store.

"You were right. You're an asshole," Simon teased him. He wasn't sure if it was the fact that Simon was older that Trevor gave him a hard time over, or just the fact that he didn't have a television. The age thing grated on his nerves. "I'm only thirty-seven. You act like I'm a grandpa or something."

Trevor's brows knitted together before he rolled his eyes. "Yeah. I get that. I'm not giving you shit over your age. Why do you always think that?"

The truth was, Simon wasn't sure. It shouldn't matter. Why should an age difference between two friends matter? But for some reason, it did. "I don't. I'm just not myself today." Speaking of which, he still felt like an ass for biting Trevor's head off when he called Simon *doctor* this morning. It still made his chest ache. Yes, he was still a doctor. He always would be. But he wasn't a *surgeon*, and that killed him.

"I only give you shit because I still can't get over the fact that you don't have a TV. I've seen you on your computer, though. You're obsessive about that, so it was a dumb joke. What the hell are you always doing on that thing, anyway?"

It was a simple question, but it made the hairs on the back of Simon's neck stand. He pretended to be writing his book. He told everyone that was his plan. He even had speech-to-text because he couldn't type much without pain. If he couldn't perform surgery, why not share his extensive knowledge of the heart with the written word?

The truth was, he hadn't started yet. He couldn't make himself. No, he spent hours on end looking up surgeries and alternate options. Test studies, and the possibility of more surgeries. He was becoming an expert at the hand and nerves, instead of the one thing he'd always loved: the heart.

Instead of answering Trevor's question, Simon said, "I owe you an apology for this morning. I shouldn't have gotten upset."

Trevor stopped in front of the sixty-four-inch televisions. "Was it the wink? It was a joke. I don't want to make you uncomfortable."

"What?" Why the hell would he think that? "No. It wasn't the wink. I've been winked at before. Jesus, do you think I'm a saint?"

Trevor seemed a little uncomfortable at that. He shuffled his feet, licked his lips, and Simon just stood there watching him. "You probably are when it comes to me. You've spent your life saving lives. I've fucked them up."

Simon waved his hand at him. A month ago, had someone else said the same thing, he wouldn't have cared either way. Let them drown in their own misery or feel guilty for things they did. He didn't have much patience for things like that, but it made the pulse in his head pound a little harder at Trevor thinking that about himself. "People can't change their pasts. All you can do is work toward the future. From what I see, you have nothing to worry about."

Heat skittered down Simon's arms at the way Trevor looked at him. The appreciation in his eyes, the way he didn't let his blue gaze drift away from him. It was like he tried to see something that Simon didn't want to show him, but almost couldn't stop it. But he could. He did. Simon stepped back. "I was an ass this morning. It's been over a year, but I'm still working through it all in my head. It's hard losing that part of me. I don't really know who I am if I'm not a surgeon." He'd put everything into it.

Trevor opened his mouth to reply but another voice spoke out before he did. "Can I help you?" Simon scrambled backward as though he'd been doing something wrong. But not Trevor. Trevor didn't move. Didn't look away. It was Simon who turned his attention toward the store employee, and as far away from Trevor as he could.

He was here to buy a television. One he would probably never watch unless it was with Trevor. "I need a television. Seventy-two inch, at least. Something with a great picture. I'm thinking a smart TV."

Trying to lighten the mood, Simon finally made himself look at Trevor…and he winked.

CHAPTER TEN

Simon decided he didn't want to mount the TV on the wall, so they made another stop by the furniture store and picked up a new entertainment center. Luckily, they'd taken Trevor's truck (Simon drove a fucking Lexus). Simon had wanted to get the thing put together and delivered, but Trevor laughed about that. Why the hell would you pay extra to have someone put together an entertainment center? Simon tried to use Trevor's hand as an excuse, but it was better now. His stitches were about to come out.

After stopping for burgers, they made their way back to Simon's house.

They'd eaten first, and now they sat in the small living room with different pieces of wood splayed out around them. "Hand me *T*. It's by your left leg." Trevor pointed toward the oak and waited for Simon to give it to him.

Simon reached for it, almost fumbled it, but quickly situated his grip. Fuck. He was stupid. Trevor's assumption was confirmed when Simon massaged his right hand with his left. "I can finish up if you—"

"I can put together an entertainment center. I'm fine."

Trevor shrugged. "I know you are." He hadn't meant that the way it sounded, but he didn't take it back, either. Maybe he should. Maybe he'd get himself into trouble, but he let Simon take that however he wanted to. Simon was an attractive man, and he wouldn't deny that he thought so. "Is there anything they can do?" he asked, getting back to the subject of Simon's hand. Another possibility with getting himself into trouble, but Trevor ignored it. He was good at that—ignoring things he shouldn't do. It had caused him too many problems to count, but he let it go since he didn't run the risk of getting addicted to Simon, or overdosing on him. He didn't think.

The right side of Simon's mouth rose, as if to say, *really?* And for the first time, Trevor noticed he had a dimple there. It made him look younger…innocent.

"Would I be sitting here if they could?"

Trevor's lips tightened.

"Shit. I didn't mean it that way. Not with you specifically."

"But it's true, whether you meant it or not. If you could perform surgery, it's what you'd be doing. You'd be in San Francisco and not here. There's nothing wrong with that. It's just a fact. I need the piece marked *U*."

Simon handed it over without a word. Trevor didn't know what in the fuck was wrong with him. He'd just taken offense to something he had no business being offended about. Things felt differently sober, that was for sure. Not just because he was moodier, but it was easier not to feel things when his emotions were dulled by whatever he'd taken that day. It wasn't like that anymore. Everything seemed to affect him now, and that pissed him off.

His skin started to feel a little too tight. Like he needed to escape. But Trevor tried to breathe through it, tried to ignore it. Less than an hour until his meeting. That was good. It would be good for him to go tonight. Just one more hour to go.

***

They didn't talk much more as they finished putting together the entertainment center. Or as Trevor put it together and Simon pretended to help.

There was a difference in Trevor. He didn't know what it was, but it became obvious as they finished up. His jaw was tighter than usual, and his movements a little more stiff. He wasn't talking or joking the way he often did, either.

It made Simon mentally stumble that he noticed such a thing. He'd never been real good at paying attention to the people in his life. Not when it came to how they felt. It wasn't only the long hours, but also Simon's obliviousness to the emotions of those around him that had killed his relationship with Heather.

"We're going to have to move this again in a few months when the remodel is done," he said as he and Trevor pushed the new piece of furniture into its spot.

"We are, huh?" There was a lightness in Trevor's voice that hadn't been there a few minutes ago.

As far as Simon…he'd said *we.* What had that been about? "Yes. You're the one who said I had to have a television, so you can help me move everything when the house is done."

They moved the television before Trevor grabbed the remote and turned it on. "Picture's good. You need satellite or cable. At least we don't have to go have pizza that tastes day-old when we want to watch something."

We. Simon wasn't the only one throwing that word around. He stepped backward. They were becoming unexpectedly close to each other. It was like spending time together was automatic, something they would do daily. What the hell was going on here?

Trevor ran a hand through his hair. Simon watched it move, and then flatten against his head again. It looked like he shaved the sides and underneath. It fit Trevor, though the haircut struck Simon as something young, he liked it.

"I need to go. My meeting is in twenty minutes. That's cutting it close." Trevor went to turn around just as Simon's right hand shot out and locked around his wrist. It was almost as though it had a mind of its own. It wouldn't work for surgery, but it worked well enough to grab Trevor without Simon instructing it to.

He needed to let go.

He really needed to let go.

Trevor's wrist was warm and rough. Hair brushed Simon's fingertips. He looked down at the skull tattoo beneath his hand. Trevor had a second skull on his upper arm. He didn't like tattoos but he found himself admiring Trevor's. "I…" He what? Simon let go. "Thanks for helping me. Oh, and for insulting my manhood because I didn't have a television." It was an attempt to lighten the mood, the mood he wasn't sure why had suddenly gotten so tense, but Trevor didn't take his bait.

"Yeah…yeah, no problem." Trevor didn't move. Didn't walk toward the door. Hadn't he said he needed to go? Simon suddenly needed him to go. "Simon..."

In that moment, there was something in the way Trevor said his name. The rough baritone of his voice. The question there. And Simon knew he would ask something that Simon didn't want to talk about. Something he wasn't sure how he would even reply to. Because he felt it, too, the tension, the connection. Christ, what the hell was this about? That word kept popping up where Trevor was concerned…connection. It was a completely unique experience for him.

"You should go. You're going to be late." His fingers still felt the rough skin of Trevor's wrist, as though they were still touching.

Trevor paused, then, "Yeah, I guess I should." But still, he didn't move, so Simon made the decision for him. He walked over to the door and opened it.

"Thanks again. I appreciate all the help. I won't be around this weekend. I'm heading into the city for the next three days to see Heather." It would be a surprise to his ex. She'd again invited him, but he'd said he couldn't make it. She was used to that, Simon not being able to make it. "I'll be back Sunday evening, so everything is a go for you guys to start on Monday."

Trevor stood by the door, staring at him. His eyes weren't as wide as they usually were. He had lines around them, the kind of lines you got not from age but from spending too much time in the sun.

"Have a good one. See you Sunday."

Simon let out a deep breath when Trevor finally responded to him, and then he was gone.

CHAPTER ELEVEN

Trevor was antsy the whole next day. He ran twice as long as he usually did, and then went to another meeting. It wasn't that he was sitting around jonesing for a drink, or thinking about trying to score some pills or anything. He just felt…edgy. It was stress-related, he was sure. Hell, maybe this would just be his life from here on out. He'd be fine for a while, and then feel like he could crawl out of his skin.

Whatever the reason, he knew going to an extra meeting couldn't hurt. It actually helped. They usually did. Afterward he went and got the stitches out of his hand.

Just as Trevor pulled into his driveway, his cell rang. He fumbled trying to pull it out of his pocket, hoping it was Simon. Whatever had happened last night needed to be forgotten. Their job started on Monday, and the last thing he wanted was any awkwardness. If he fucked this up for Blake and the crew, he would never forgive himself.

It was more than that, though… Simon was his friend. Hell, he couldn't remember having many of those. People he got drunk or high with didn't count. They weren't really his friends. They were people he partied with. There was a big difference, though he hadn't known it at the time. Back then, Trevor would have called them friends. It was only after getting clean that he realized none of them were to be found.

But it wasn't Simon. It was his mom, and guilt poked and prodded at his insides as Trevor considered not answering. He loved his mom. She loved Trevor and Blake both. No matter what he'd done in his life, she never lost faith in him, and that counted for a whole hell of a lot.

It's what made it so hard to look at her.

Trevor hit TALK. "Hey, Mom."

"Hey, mom? All I get is a 'hey, Mom'? Geez, we live in the same town and I haven't seen you in close to a month. You've been quite the busy bee lately. How's your hand?"

Trevor rolled his truck window down to let in some of the warm, late-Spring air. Spring and Summer were his favorite times of the year. "It's good. I got my stitches out today. Everything healed just fine. We're starting a new job on Monday."

"I know. Your brother told me. Out at the old Stoneridge property, right? He was proud of you, ya know. Getting that job for Rock Solid. I'm so proud of both of you boys."

Trevor tried to smile. "Thanks, Mom." There was no reason for her words to bother him, but they did. Trevor landing the job had been a surprise to everyone. He knew Blake had every right to doubt him. Trevor knew he'd screwed up too many times to count. He'd done many more wrongs than rights in his life, but it still sucked that something as little as landing a job was a reason for them to be proud of him. If it had been Blake, it would be expected that he get it. With Trevor, it was an accomplishment.

“I talked to Blake on his lunch break. I told him I want you boys to come over for dinner tomorrow night. Jason might come, too. Your brother said he wasn’t sure if you could make it, you’ve had so much going on. I want to see your face. Can you come?”

“Hey, Blake will be there. That means you get to see my face. Why do you need me there?” The words had rolled out without being planned. “I’m sorry. It’s been a long day. I didn’t mean that. Of course I’ll be there.”

There was a pause on the line. Without seeing her, Trevor knew his mom’s mind was running, overthinking Trevor’s outburst, because once you’re an addict, you can’t just have a bad day. It’s because you are coming down, or in need of something. You can’t just have plans with a friend where you go jogging with him, eat pizza and put together an entertainment center, you have to be out partying.

And he got it. He did. Trevor deserved that. He didn’t have anyone to blame other than himself. That didn’t make it any easier to deal with, and right now, he didn’t have it in him to assure her he was fine.

“I’ll be there. I need to run, though. I have some errands to take care of today.”

“Okay…I love you, Trevor.”

“I love you too, Mom.” Trevor hung up the phone and wondered what in the hell he would do with his day.

***

“I can’t believe you decided to come.” Heather kept close to him as they made their way down the beach.

"I needed to get away. Things will be busy with the upcoming remodel. If I didn't come now, it would be months before I had the chance." Really, that wouldn't have mattered. He wouldn't have come because of that.

Heather wrapped her arm around Simon's waist and gave him a half hug. She was a hugger. She'd always been that way. The first day they'd met in college, she'd hugged him. Simon hadn't known what to think about that. Eventually, he'd gotten used to Heather's affection, but it still felt awkward at times.

She was a surgeon's daughter. She understood all the long hours and hard work. In the beginning, Heather hardly ever complained, and that had worked for Simon. She was exactly what he'd needed in a woman: smart, kind, understanding, and independent. She had plans of her own, so she understood Simon's.

It wasn't that he didn't love her. He had. He still did. No, Simon wasn't *in* love with Heather anymore, but he did love her. But even from the beginning, he'd been very aware of how well they would work. She didn't get mad at him if he went a few days without calling. If he was so busy studying that he forgot her birthday. Because she'd known it wasn't that he didn't care about her. What he did just meant that much to him. He'd always wanted to save lives. He'd always wanted to fix hearts.

They'd been engaged by his senior year. It would be a while before they married. She got that. School came first.

They were married a couple years later. Things went well during his residency. He'd blown people away, being so young yet so good at what he did. He was hardly settled into his career by the time she wanted to have a baby.

Simon hadn't. It wasn't the right time. They had too much going on.

Like she always did, Heather understood. It was a year later that she started to tell him how lonely she was. How much she missed him.

Six months later, they started trying to get pregnant.

Six months after that, she didn't understand why it hadn't happened yet. He'd told her it would take time. Simon still worked a lot. He worked nights at times. He wasn't always there when she was ovulating.

When another six months passed, they went to see a doctor.

It hadn't been her, it had been him. They could always adopt. She could use a sperm donor, yada, yada. They would think about it. Discuss their options.

Simon didn't stop working. He worked more. Even when he wasn't at work, he was still studying the heart. Learning more about it.

Heather wasn't so understanding anymore. She wanted her husband. She wanted a baby.

Simon couldn't give her either of them. The first was more of a choice than the second. The divorce came a short time later.

They were closer now as friends than they had been when they were married. Sometimes he missed her. Wished he could give her what she needed, but he couldn't. Not then and not even now, because it didn't matter if he could perform surgery or not, it was still what held his heart.

"How are you doing?" she asked as they continued to walk.

Simon sighed. He knew that was coming. “Fine.”

“Try again. I know you, remember? I was married to you.”

He looked at her and grinned. “But you’re not anymore, which means I don’t have to talk about my feelings if I don’t want to.”

Heather laughed. “Please. Like that’s any different. Even when we were married you never talked to me. Not about how you really felt.”

It was the truth, and that made him an asshole. “I’m sorry.”

“I know you are. You introduced me to Alan, so you’re forgiven. Plus, you’re not only that way with me, you’re that way with everyone. That makes it easier.”

She set her head on his shoulder as they walked, and Simon knew she wasn’t done yet. “I think you should try again. Just because it didn’t work the first time, doesn’t mean surgery isn’t still an option for you. I—”

“It’s no use,” Simon cut her off. Logically he knew she was right, but emotionally, getting his hopes up scared him. “It is what it is, sweetheart. I don’t want to talk about it. I came here to get away for a few days. Let’s just try and enjoy it.”

She nodded, and he realized that it didn’t matter that they weren’t married anymore. He still managed to break the one organ he was supposed to know the most about. Her heart.

CHAPTER TWELVE

"Jason isn't coming?" his mom asked when they walked through the door of their childhood home. It was a small, modest house. Only two bedrooms. He and Blake had shared their whole lives. Their father died of liver disease in the room his mom still slept in.

"Yeah, Blake. No Jason?" Trevor cocked a brow at his twin, aware that he was behaving like a teenager, even though he wasn't sure why.

The truth was, Trevor wasn't surprised they didn't end up being serious about each other. They were best friends who decided to be friends with benefits for a short time. Mom always assumed they would end up together, and she'd thought that was that. They decided to be friends again, she thought it meant they broke up but it didn't change their friendship. Everyone loved Blake. Everyone wanted to be his friend.

"Ha ha, big brother. What about you? No Simon?"

Fuck. Their mom looked back and forth between the two of them. "Wait. Who is Simon? Are you seeing someone?" Her voice was a high-pitched mix of hope and fear. He had no doubt she would love to see both of them happy with a partner, but she would always worry about whomever Trevor ended up with. Worry he would screw it up, take things badly, and start using again if they broke up.

"No, Mom. I'm not seeing anyone. We're only friends. Blake's just giving me a hard time." He wasn't sure why he didn't add in the fact that Simon was straight and currently with his ex-wife, an hour and a half away in San Francisco.

Blake raised a brow at Trevor as if to say, *how do you like it? Give me shit and I'll give it right back, only you'll get it a lot worse than me.* Because he would. There would only be the hope if it came to Blake finding someone. There would be no fear in sight.

Trevor flipped his brother off behind his mom's back. Blake barked out a laugh, and then their mom was looking back and forth between the two of them again.

"I always feel like I'm missing something when it comes to the two of you." He heard the love in her words. It made Trevor have to look away. The heavy ache he always had in the center of his chest grew. It hurt looking at her. Hurt knowing how much pain she'd endured because of him. Their father hadn't treated her the way he should have, and then Trevor had broken her heart over and over again.

"It smells good in here! Smells like Italian," he tried to change the subject but his eyes caught Blake's. His brother cocked his head questioningly.

Trevor shook his head, trying to tell him that he was fine.

Dinner went well. His mom was a much better cook than Trevor was. The three of them sat at the table together and talked about Rock

Solid, summer plans, Jason, and whatever safe topics they could think to talk about. Trevor felt guilty that they didn't do this more often. It was a good night. He knew it wouldn't last, though. They'd just gotten into Blake's truck when his brother said, "She's been worried. With the injury and you having time off."

Idle hands are the devil's play thing...

"I'm fine. You know I'm fine. You'd know if I wasn't. Did you tell her?"

"I did," he confirmed. "She needs to hear it more often from you, though. I know it's a hassle sometimes. I know she's overprotective, but it's just because she loves you. You need to call her and go see her more often."

Oh, fuck. Here they went again. "Yes, Dad."

"Screw you, Trev. I'm not trying to be a dick. I'm just trying to be supportive. She's our mom. If you can make time to hang out with *Simon* all the time, then you can see her now and again."

Trevor turned his brother's way in the darkened truck. "What the fuck is your problem with him?"

At first he didn't think Blake was going to respond, but then he jerked over to the side of the road and hit the interior light. "My problem with him? Nothing. I don't even know the guy."

Trevor bit his bottom lip and ran a hand through his hair. *Rock Solid, mom, meetings, sobriety...* "So that means your problem is with me? I get it. I do. But if you didn't want to do this, if you weren't sure about getting a place with me or opening the business with me, you should have said so earlier. I know I've given you every reason not to trust me, but—"

"It's not that…"

Yeah, right.

"Okay, it's not *only* that, it's just…do you think it's a good idea? Seeing this guy? I mean, is it the best time to get involved? Is it smart to get involved with someone who we're going to be under contract with for the next several months?"

So that's what this was about. Trevor tried to ignore the fact that there had been some kind of…awkwardness between him and Simon the last time they'd seen each other. It was probably all from Trevor's side, and he could curb that. He could. "He's straight, man. He went to visit his ex-wife this weekend. I'm not going to fuck the guy and make us lose this contract. I promise you, I'm *not* going to screw this up." It sucked that Blake had every right to fear that Trevor would make a mess of things.

"Then why? Hell, you're with the guy every day."

He shrugged. This was the tricky part. "We're friends. It works, hanging out with him."

"It never used to matter that I'm your brother. I've always been your friend, too. Jason, JT and Andrea. We're all your friends."

Friends. They were Blake's friends, who were cool with Trevor because of Blake. Trevor leaned forward with his elbows on the dashboard and his head in his hands. "Do you remember that time I was supposed to go help Bob move?" He was their mom's boyfriend for a short time. It was the only time she dated. They'd broken up because of Trevor. "But I went out and got really fucked up the night before. I brought some guys with me to help, and one of them ended up stealing a bunch of shit from him, and I didn't notice. I was too fucked up to get it, and it broke Mom's heart. Bob told her she was too soft on me and she broke it off with him. You stuck up for me even though you knew it was my screw up. I brought them around, people I didn't know and only got high with, and they robbed the man."

Blake's voice cracked when he said, "Yeah. I remember."

"There are a hundred stories like that. You know them, and Mom knows them. Jason, JT, Andrea, they all know them. Half the people in Rockford Falls knows them. Simon doesn't. He's the only person who doesn't have those memories of me. He's the only one who doesn't have judgment in his eyes, no matter how right it would be. It feels good to be around someone who only sees this Trevor when they look at me, and not the one I'm trying my hardest not to be."

He didn't look at his brother. Couldn't. His chest hurt too much.

It was a long time before Blake spoke. "I don't mean to look at you that way."

"I know," Trevor replied. And he did know that. "But that doesn't change the fact that you do, just like no matter how far I go, it will never change what I've done."

***

"Alan asked me to marry him. I said yes." Simon's fork fell out of his hand at Heather's statement. He wasn't sure why it surprised him so much. It shouldn't. They'd been together for a while now. They worked well together.

She was that independent woman again because she knew Alan

loved her. He was a successful, highly respected doctor, but he still never put that above Heather.

"Wow." He picked up his fork again. "That's great." Jesus, why the hell did those words sound so forced?

"You sound like you're constipated," she said dryly.

"You're not my doctor or my wife. There's no reason we should discuss my digestive tract." Simon took a drink of wine. It reminded him of Trevor and he set the glass back down. It had been easy for him not to drink around his friend. He wasn't much of a drinker, and now he felt almost guilty for having a glass. "I'm happy for you, sweetheart. I really am. You deserve someone who treats you right."

Heather smiled at him, her eyes wet with unshed tears. "Thank you. Your opinion means the world to me, Simon. We didn't work out, but I spent some of the best years of my life with you. You're my best friend, which is why, despite knowing it will piss you off, I'm going to tell you that you deserve someone too. I want you to be able to operate again. I want that more than anything, but you have to know…it's not the only thing out there."

Each of her words were a knife into his chest, ripping him open.

"You're a smart man, but just because you're smart doesn't mean your brain is all you need to use. You've spent years working on other people's hearts…what about your own?"

Simon tossed his napkin on the table and leaned back. "Romance is the last thing on my mind right now."

"Ha! Like that's new! It's always been the last thing on your mind. I'm pretty sure you approached our relationship more like a business proposition than love."

Had he done that? Had he really?

"We got along great for the most part, and we both know the sex was good."

He caught Heather's eye and she smiled. She was right, it had been.

"But you married me because you thought it would be easy. My dad was a doctor, and you knew you would always be married to your work. And if that's what you want, you still can be. Surgery or not—"

"I'm a surgeon, Heather."

"Yes, you are. And you're a cardiologist. You can still practice. Or don't. Write your book if you want, but you need to stop wasting away. Meet someone. Have a one-night stand, fall in love, find another surgeon who thinks they can fix your hand. Just do *something.*"

This conversation was entirely too emotional for him. "How do you know I haven't had a one night stand?"

She rolled her eyes. "This isn't about sex. It's about your life. You deserve to be happy, Simon. Alan has this friend, Debbie..."

"Jesus. No. No way. Don't you think it's a little strange that you're marrying one of my old business colleagues and now you're trying to set me up with his friend? I'm fine. There's nothing wrong with me. I'm writing my book and renovating a home. I'm fine," he said again. But he wasn't fine. Not really.

CHAPTER THIRTEEN

Two weeks into the remodel and Trevor had hardly spoken to Simon. It wasn't that they were unfriendly or anything. Simon would get progress reports on the house, or stop by to check things out as they worked. He finally met Blake, so some of the back and forth went through his brother now (even though he still went to Trevor first). And maybe it should. Maybe Blake had been right. If they hardly spoke just because they stood too close to each other and Simon held his wrist, being friends while doing this remodel would be a huge mistake.

Or maybe he'd just been reading too much into the friendship. They hung out for a few weeks and now they didn't. Shit like that happened all the time.

So, Trevor moved on with his life. What else did he have to do? He started hitting up more meetings because sitting around the house drove him bat shit crazy. He got up earlier every day so he could run before work. It was dark half the time he was out there, but he didn't mind that. He liked it when the rest of the world was asleep. A year and a half ago, he would have just been going to bed, if he'd slept at all.

"Hey, I've been thinking about getting up early with you to go running." Blake filled his insulated coffee cup and snapped the lid on.

"Yeah?" Trevor asked. That would be cool. He liked the idea of having that time with his brother. They worked together, and saw each other at home, but they didn't hang out. He missed that. He missed not feeling alone.

"I'm not making any promises." He laughed. "It's early as hell, but I'll try. I'll show you up out there, big brother."

This time it was Trevor's turn to laugh. "Keep dreaming, little brother."

But yeah, he liked the idea. It would give them a chance to really work on getting to know each other again. Before Trevor lost himself, he was always with his brother.

But Blake didn't get up to run with him the next day, or any day that week. He joked about how he tried every day but the snooze button kept magically pushing itself.

And it made sense to Trevor. Getting up at four-thirty in the morning wasn't for everyone. But it disappointed him too.

***

In the past month, Simon had become addicted to YouTube. He watched it instead of researching. He watched it instead of writing his book. He watched it instead of doing much of anything, and thanks to Trevor, he was able to watch it on an app on his television.

There were millions of videos out there on heart surgery, interviews with patients and doctors. Experimental procedures. All of it.

He watched and critiqued. Watched and wished like hell it was him.

It gave him something to do.

And if Simon were being honest, he would admit those weren't the only videos he watched. He'd suddenly become obsessed with cooking shows, of all things. They didn't help. He burned half of what he made or it tasted like shit, but again, it gave him something to focus on.

He was being ridiculous. There wasn't a part of Simon in denial about that. There was no reason to keep his distance from Trevor. What had happened (or didn't happen) really wasn't a big deal. That single moment in time where the tension between them had spiked and Simon had been unable to let go of Trevor's hand wasn't what had driven distance between them, anyway.

It was Heather.

Simon couldn't get her words out of his head. He'd never done right by her. He had been married to his work more than he ever had been to her.

She was wrong that he needed to move on, though. How could he? Not when he loved something so much. He didn't need a one-night-stand or to fall in love. He just needed to get back the piece of Simon that made him *Simon*.

He needed to get back to being Dr. Simon Malone, Cardio-Thoracic Surgeon. It was the only thing he wanted, and getting involved with someone would just make things more difficult.

Only, he wasn't doing anything to make that happen, either. The truth was, he could try another surgery. If one didn't work the likelihood of the next wasn't great, but he could try.

And he *was* lonely. He'd never felt that until this last year of his life. As much of a prick as it made him, not even when Heather left.

But now, it was even more intensified. That was the why of the cooking. He was lonely, and thinking of why made sweat bead on Simon's forehead and his chest feel heavy.

He missed something other than just his career. He missed a person.

CHAPTER FOURTEEN

"It's Friday. We should all do something. Blake, Trev? You guys in?" Jason ripped out a beam, letting the wood crash to the floor. "I need to get laid."

"Nice. Gay or straight, men are such pigs," Andrea called out, and everyone except Trevor laughed. Was Jason mental? In what world was it a good idea for him to ask Trevor to go out with him?

"Come on, Andrea. You love being let in on the male mind. You have three gay men and a straight guy at your disposal all day. Don't women want to know how we think?" Jason grinned at her.

It was JT who replied. "Hey! Keep me out of this! I'm married."

Trevor took a sledgehammer and swung, beating holes into a wall he was trying to knock down.

"Sorry about your luck," Jason teased him before continuing. "What do you guys think? A night out sounds fun, especially for you, you hermit." He eyed Trevor. "I was kidding about the laid part. We can go catch a movie and have dinner or something."

Trevor swung the hammer again, flicking a glance over his shoulder in time to see Jason and Blake make eye contact. Ah, so that's what this was about. His brother had told Jason that Trevor needed out of the house, so Jase was doing Blake's dirty work for him. "Shut up. Like the two of you want to go have dinner and see a movie with me." That wasn't a typical night out. He didn't want to make it sound like they went out all the time or anything, but he just couldn't see Jase wanting to hit up a show with them.

"We used to do that all the time." Blake raised a brow at him. If he wanted to spend time with Trevor, there were other ways. The morning runs could be one of them.

"When we were sixteen, because he had nothing better to do." Trevor wiped the sweat from his forehead.

"That's not true. Jase and I go see a movie sometimes. It's just—" Blake shook his head. "Never mind."

Oh, yeah. It was Trevor's fault again. Once Trevor started drinking and using, he hadn't wanted to do anything like that.

"No fighting, boys." Jason shook a teasing finger at them. "He's probably right though, B. It's not a movie he needs. We can get you laid without hitting up a bar, Trev."

Trevor wasn't in the mood, but he couldn't help but laugh.

"It always comes back to sex with you, doesn't it?" Blake threw a piece of drywall at Jase.

"And that's a bad thing, why?" Jason replied.

The two of them would go on for days if Trevor didn't interrupt. "I appreciate the offer, but I don't need you guys to babysit me or to drag me out of the house. I'm fine. If I want to see a movie, I'll go see one. If I want to get laid, I'll find someone to fuck. I'm a big boy."

"Or, you know, maybe we just want to spend time with you. That's an option too." Jason shook his head, looking frustrated.

Trevor felt like all the wood they'd pulled down was now piled on his back. Shit. They were right. There was no reason he couldn't hang out with his brother and his brother's best friend. Just as Trevor opened his mouth to say so, another voice cut in. "This open space is going to work much better."

Simon.

Trevor sighed. He was annoyed now. Annoyed at himself, at Blake and Jason, and at Simon too. "Yeah, it'll give you a lot of room."

Blake raised a brow at Trevor. Yeah, he knew. Simon shouldn't be in here. Not right now. Half the time his brother didn't trust Trevor to deal with things, but he obviously wanted Trevor to be the one to deal with Simon, which worked since Simon had said he wanted Trevor to run this. A fact he hadn't told his brother about. "It's dangerous to be here without any protective equipment."

Half of Simon's mouth kicked up and Trevor could read his expression. *What? I might cut my hand on a nail?*

"Shut up." Trevor shook his head, but he was smiling.

"Trev," Blake said just as Simon replied, "I didn't say anything." And he was smiling too.

"Do you have a minute? I'd like to get your thoughts on an idea I had about the house." Simon wasn't looking at anyone in the room other than Trevor.

Trevor held back a groan, though he wasn't really sure why he felt that way. If it was the fact that it felt good to see Simon when it shouldn't, or something else. He didn't really have to have a reason to be in a bad mood anymore.

"Yeah, sure. I'm coming." Trevor took off his hardhat and set it down before scratching his head.

He didn't look at his brother or anyone else in the room as he followed Simon outside. He wore a pair of jeans that hugged his long legs, and a T-shirt. "I don't have much time. The guy we're working for is a real hard-ass." He hoped Simon would laugh at that, and he got his wish.

Simon sat on the porch steps. Trevor stalled a minute and then joined him. "I always loved this house," he found himself saying. It was old. It reminded Trevor of an old farmhouse in the South, with shutters on the windows and a wraparound porch. "When I was a kid I used to dream about riding a dirt bike in all that open space out back." That was another thing he'd forgotten about until the words found their way out of his mouth.

"It's beautiful. I knew I had to have it when I saw it. It's supposed to be inspiring me to write." Simon's words pulled him out of his thoughts.

"How's that working for you?" He knew the answer to that. Simon wasn't writing.

"I'm waiting for the guy I hired to do the remodel to finish. He's a real slow-ass." Simon winked at him. Trevor rested his elbows on his knees, his feet two steps below the one he sat on.

"They're taking you out to get laid tonight, I hear."

"No, they're trying to babysit me. If they go do anything it's not going to be at a place where no alcohol is sold." It wasn't that they were big partiers, but they enjoyed going out, drinking and dancing sometimes. Or drinking and fucking. Hell, even if they went to a game or something there would be beer. It wasn't that Trevor was never around it—people drank at restaurants when he went out to dinner—but his friends or brother never did it around him. If he went, they would curb what they did. "I don't want to be a downer on their night."

Simon stood but Trevor didn't move. He watched, though. He kept his eyes on Simon the whole time. "Come over tonight. I've been watching cooking shows on YouTube. I'll make you dinner."

Trevor leaned back, and let his legs stretch out on the steps. "You any good?"

"Nope, but I have a high-quality television. It's good for more than just the internet."

Trevor barked out a laugh. "You should thank the guy who took you shopping for it."

But Simon didn't. He only said, "See you at seven," and then headed back to the small house.

Trevor didn't move for a few minutes. He didn't know what in the hell that had been about, or what caused the change of heart. Simon obviously hadn't wanted to talk to him about the house.

Trevor knew he'd go tonight. There wasn't a chance he wouldn't go.

As soon as he made it back upstairs, Jason said, "Let me guess? You have plans tonight now?"

Trevor didn't look at him when he replied, "He's straight, you asshole." And even though he had no business thinking it, Trevor wished he wasn't.

***

At five after seven, there was a knock at Simon's door. He pushed off the couch and went to let Trevor in. It's funny how people being late bothered him, even if it was only a few minutes, yet it didn't with Trevor.

"Hello." Simon held the door while Trevor came in.

"I brought some wine."

Simon felt his eyes go wide but saw the joke in Trevor's. "You're an asshole."

"So I've been told. It smells good."

"It probably won't be." Simon closed the door. "I made lasagna."

"Fancy." Trevor cocked a brow at him.

"Hey." Simon grabbed ahold of Trevor's arm when he went to walk away.

"Don't." Trevor shook his head. "It's cool."

Even though he shouldn't, he accepted Trevor's way out of an apology. He wasn't very good at those anyway.

"Have you been running?" Trevor sat at the table.

"Yeah, I'm still at it. You?" It had only been a month since they hung out, but somehow it felt longer than that. Simon sat across from Trevor.

"Yep. I go early so I can get it in before work. Blake was going to start going with me but he never drags himself out of bed."

"It's funny how quickly I got used to going with someone else. The run feels longer on your own."

Trevor shrugged. "We can go together again if you're up for it. Like I said, I'm out there early. But it might be difficult. You'd probably have to come into town to go with me. It would be tight time-wise for me to drive out here, run, then go back home and shower before coming back for work."

What the hell was with the tension in the air? It was awkward and stifling. Trevor didn't seem to feel it, but Simon did. It reminded him of how he should have felt with Heather when they broke up and then spent time together. Only it never happened.

Broke up? What are you thinking, Simon?

The timer went off and Simon actually twitched. He felt completely out of his element here, but couldn't put his finger on why.

"You okay?" Trevor's forehead wrinkled when his brows pulled together like they did.

No, he wasn't okay. He didn't think. Or maybe he was. Really, he didn't even know what they were doing here. Dinner was obvious, but he hadn't had a plan when he'd gone to the house to talk to Trevor, yet here they were.

"I'm fine." Simon stood and went to the stove. He pulled the lasagna from the oven, and then set out plates for them. The table was small, so they wouldn't have room for it there.

A second later he heard Trevor moving around behind him. He pulled the tea from the fridge without Simon offering it to him, as though he felt that comfortable in Simon's home.

They made their plates and poured their drinks without a word. It was only a couple minutes later that they were back in their spots at the table.

"Looks good." Trevor dug into his lasagna and loaded his fork with a bite. Simon did the same, and then they both took a bite and… *Crunch.* "I think the pasta could have cooked a little longer."

Shit. He knew this was a bad idea. Simon tried to finish chewing, but lasagna with half-crunchy noodles was not his thing. "What the hell? Why didn't they cook?"

"Did you boil them first?" Trevor asked.

No. Simon didn't answer.

"Did you buy the pasta that you don't have to boil ahead of time?"

No. Again, Simon didn't answer.

"I hope you were a better surgeon than you are a cook."

Simon's first response was to freeze up. To tell Trevor to fuck off. He was the best surgeon there was. That's not what came out when he opened his mouth, though. No, it was a laugh. A second later Trevor was laughing too. Both men were pushing their plates away from them, as they continued laughing.

And just like that, the tension didn't bear down on Simon anymore. For the first time in a while, he felt good.

For the first time in a month, if he was being honest.

CHAPTER FIFTEEN

Since the lasagna didn't work out so well, they ordered pizza. It was the only food they could get delivered, and then they'd started a movie and watched things blow up.

Trevor was more aware than he should be of Simon sitting on the other side of the couch. He realized he had his feet on Simon's coffee table and immediately put them down on the floor like Simon's. It was kind of an asshole move to kick his feet up at someone else's house like that.

"Its okay. This isn't the furniture I'm keeping anyway." Simon called him out on what he'd been thinking.

He almost teased Simon about his need for the best of everything but he didn't. Instead, Trevor watched the credits on the screen and said, "I should go." But he didn't move. The couch dipped. Simon must be changing positions, but Trevor didn't look at him. He didn't want to go. For the first time in a month, he didn't feel alone, and he wanted that feeling to stay.

"My ex-wife is now engaged to an old colleague of mine. She told me when I went into the city."

Trevor couldn't help but look his way at that. It was a reminder, the fact that Simon had an ex-wife. When he did turn, he saw Simon relaxed, his head against the back of the couch, but turned toward Trevor, looking at him. There was pain in his wide, gray eyes, and that made Trevor feel the same. He'd gotten too close. For the first time in his life he'd gotten close enough to a man to care, even if it was only friendship, yet that couldn't be true, either. Because he was hurt at Simon's pain over his ex wife.

That could be considered a friendship thing, though, couldn't it? People didn't want to see their friends hurt. Since being sober, half of the time he felt confused about his feelings because they weren't dull anymore. "I'm sorry."

"It's strange, because on the one hand, I'm okay with it. I want her happy. I love her. She's a good friend to me and she's a good person. We don't belong together. I know that as well as she does. I could never give her what she wants. School and work were always more important to me than Heather was. When we were married, she wanted a baby so badly—a little part of us, she would say. It didn't happen, and then we found out it likely never would. It wrecked her. Broke her, and…I was thankful… I was thankful, because how could I be the surgeon I needed to be if we had a child? What kind of man feels that way?"

Christ, he wanted to reach out for Simon. Wanted so bad to reach out and touch him. "We all feel things we sometimes shouldn't. We all make mistakes. It makes us human. I've stolen money from my own mother for drugs. I sold Blake's mountain bike without his permission for drugs. If we're all held accountable for our mistakes in the past, I'm fucked."

"But that's the thing." Simon closed his eyes and took a deep breath. "You're changing. You're making amends. I'm not. I would still choose my career over being married to Heather. I still wouldn't give her a baby, even if I could. Above anything else, I want my hand to work the way it should. There is nothing I would choose over being a heart surgeon, and I look at men like Alan. Men that can marry, that make their wives happy, raise children and not put their career over them, and it baffles my mind. My brain doesn't work that way. That's what makes me wrong."

In that moment, Trevor wasn't sure he'd ever felt closer to another human being. They were so different in so many ways…but so similar in others. "There isn't a day that goes by that I don't consider giving up. That I don't miss it. That I don't think about how much easier it would be to disappear, leave Mom and Blake behind and spend my life drinking and partying it away." That was a truth he'd never told another soul. There were times he didn't know if he wanted to stay clean.

"But you don't. That's the difference, Trevor. You don't. You do the right thing because you know how to love people."

They were closer somehow. He didn't know if it was himself who'd moved or Simon. He thought maybe it was both of them, they'd both somehow drifted toward one another.

"I'm sorry. I freaked out that last night and I'm not entirely sure why. I shouldn't have, and I owe you an apology. You've been a good friend, and I missed you." Simon closed his eyes and Trevor's whole body surged with energy. "I'm not sure I've ever told anyone I missed them before," Simon added.

Trevor didn't stop to think. He followed every impulse in his body and leaned forward and pressed his mouth to Simon's. The second their lips touched, Simon's immediately opened up for him. Trevor dipped his tongue into Simon's mouth. Suddenly he needed *more, more, more.* More of everything, so he kissed deeper, harder. He let his hands grab the side of Simon's face. It was smooth like it always was, and that damned square jaw of his fit just right beneath Trevor's cupped hand.

He let it slide down, slipped it under Simon's shirt as he moved closer, and that's when the mouth beneath his stopped moving and Simon jerked away.

Fuck.

He'd gone off his instinct, acted without thinking. Again, for the millionth time in his life, Trevor knew he fucked up.

***

"Shit! I'm sorry. I shouldn't have done that. Christ. What was I thinking? You were just talking to me about your wife and I kiss you?"

Yeah, Trevor kissed him, and Simon had kissed him back. Simon wanted to do it again. Wanted to feel the press of the stud in Trevor's lip dig into his.

"It won't happen again. You're my friend. I won't take advantage of that." Trevor pushed to his feet. "It won't happen again," he said for the second time.

As he tried to walk away, Simon reached out for him, wrapped his hand around Trevor's wrist the way he had the last time they spent time together.

"You're straight. I had no business kissing you. I know that." But Trevor didn't take his hand back and Simon didn't let go.

Simon said, "That wasn't a first for me." And he didn't want it to be a last, either. It was probably the worst idea he ever had, but he wanted Trevor's mouth on his again. He wanted to let go, to forget. To lose himself in someone else. He'd already lost himself, but at least if he did it here, with Trevor, he would enjoy it. They'd be lost together. Half the time it felt like that anyway.

"What do you mean it's not a first for you?" The shock in Trevor's voice made him smile.

"College. I was working my ass off in school and didn't want anything serious. There were a few men back then. I guess you can call me bi-sexual. I never put much thought into it. I just knew I enjoyed both men and women when I took the time away from studying to have some fun. Then I met Heather, and it was only her after that. There wasn't any reason to think about it much after her. But I'm thinking about it now, and I want you."

"Why didn't you tell me?"

"It's not usually my conversation starter. And I thought we were just friends. I'm telling you I want you now, though."

That's all it took to persuade Trevor. He jerked his arm, and Simon went easily. He stood, and then their mouths crashed down on each other. Their teeth clanked together. It was frantic and messy and unskilled, but Simon didn't care. In this moment he wasn't the man who broke Heather's heart. He wasn't the surgeon with a fucked up hand. He was only a man, a man taking and receiving pleasure.

Trevor's mouth slid down to Simon's neck. Trevor's rough facial hair and the piercing rubbed against him. "Jesus, you could have told me that a long time ago. How far?" Trevor shoved his hands under Simon's shirt and pushed it up. Simon finished pulling it over his own head.

"You're chatty. Are you asking me how far I've gone with other men?"

Trevor chuckled against his skin before he ran his tongue over Simon's flat nipple.

"No, I'm asking you how far you can throw a baseball. Of course I'm asking you how far you've gone. Or at least what you like."

Simon froze up at that. Yes, there had been other men, but he'd never been fucked. It wasn't something he was opposed to, he didn't think, but he wasn't ready for that tonight. Plus, "I am so out of the loop. I don't have condoms. Do you?" He wanted to laugh again. As he ran his hands up and down Trevor's back, wishing he'd taken Trevor's shirt off. He felt like a horny teenager, freaking out because he didn't have protection. He couldn't remember the last time he'd felt this way.

"Okay, so no fucking. I really want your dick in my mouth, though." Trevor palmed Simon's erection through his pants and Simon moaned. "And mine in yours. I'll jerk us off together too. We should hurry. There's a lot to do."

There was another laugh from Simon. He couldn't help it, and then his hands were on Trevor's face. He felt the man's short beard against his palms. He rubbed it, let it prick into his skin as he kissed Trevor. It was Simon leading this time. Him pushing his tongue into Trevor's mouth. Simon taking a step forward so he could get to the bedroom. That forward step was a backward one for Trevor, and then…"Oh, shit."

Simon caught Trevor as he almost fell over the coffee table. They were both like inexperienced virgins needing to get off. It had been a long time, close to two years since Simon had an orgasm with anyone other than himself.

"I'm not usually so bad at this. In fact, I'm usually pretty damn good at it. I just…" He wanted Trevor so fucking much. He didn't usually say things like that…though it seems he did with Trevor. He'd told him tonight that he wanted him and missed him. That was huge for Simon.

"I want you, too." Trevor kissed him slowly this time. There wasn't the same urgency to it, but the passion was still there. He kissed Simon's neck again, down his chest, only he didn't stop. Trevor pushed the table out of the way with his foot, and then kneeled, kissing Simon's stomach.

His fingers worked the button and zipper on Simon's pants as he continued kissing and biting at Simon's stomach. Simon ran a hand through Trevor's hair the way Trevor did to himself a hundred times a day.

Trevor's hands shoved down the back of his pants. First, Trevor cupped his ass and he could swear his knees went weak. Next Trevor shoved his jeans and underwear down. Then his mouth was back, kissing the crease where Simon's leg met his hip.

He looked down at him, this broad, sexy man on his knees, who leaned forward and buried his face in Simon's crotch, in his pubic hair, breathing him in.

"Suck me," Simon managed to grit out. "Please, suck me."

His whole body shuddered when Trevor did exactly what he asked.

CHAPTER SIXTEEN

Trevor had always been really good about turning off the logical part of his brain. He was good at ignoring it, and just doing what he wanted, and this was no different. It didn't matter that they were doing a remodel for Simon, and it didn't matter that they were friends. That Simon hadn't touched a man since college, and that this could ruin their friendship. Later, it would matter. Later, it would hurt like hell, but *right now*, he just did what he wanted.

And he wanted Simon.

Trevor reached up, tested the weight of Simon's balls in his hand as he sucked Simon's crown into his mouth. He didn't take him deep. Not at first. He just teased the end, hollowing his cheeks out for suction.

"Holy shit. Jesus fucking Christ," Simon mumbled above him, and Trevor smiled around the head of Simon's cock.

See what you've been missing? he wanted to tell him. *When I told you I was gay, you could have told me you liked men, too. We could have been doing this the whole time.*

But he hadn't, and that was another thing Trevor didn't want to think about—the *why* of it. Instead, he focused on what he was doing, and took Simon deep this time. He inhaled, taking in the musky smell of him before pulling off and then swallowing him down again.

He wanted Simon's ass. Wanted Simon to have his too. Wanted to fuck Simon's mouth and let Simon fuck his, because Simon wasn't fucking him. Right now he was letting Trevor lead the blowjob.

Trevor let Simon's dick slip out of his mouth with a *pop* before going lower, and sucking each of Simon's balls, first the left, then the right. They hung low, and he always fucking loved that, low-hanging balls.

He moved back to Simon's cock, sucking him again, playing with Simon's sac as he did.

"Trev…that feels so good. I'm going to come if you keep going."

It was the first time Simon called him Trev. It suggested a level of intimacy they hadn't touched before, and he wanted that too, the sound of his name on Simon's lips along with his come. "That's the point. Do it. Want to taste you."

He sucked the head with deep pulls again.

"Oh fuck. Don't say things like that. I don't want to lose it yet."

Trevor sucked hard. He let his hand travel back, tracing the crease of Simon's ass with his fingers.

"You said…fuck, that feels good…you said you wanted…to jerk...us off...together."

Trevor pulled off and looked up at Simon, who looked down at him.

"You want to come together? How sweet. See? You are a romantic."

Simon playfully pushed Trevor's head. "Fuck off."

"Us off. Us, remember?" Trevor stood and got rid of his clothes as quickly as he could. "Sit down," he told Simon, who did. He could tell that much like the rest of his life, Simon wasn't used to doing what he was told in the bedroom. But still, this was his first time with a man in a long time, and he seemed to need Trevor to take the lead on it.

Trevor didn't mind.

"I like the nipple piercing," Simon said.

Trevor cocked a brow. "We can do yours too." There wasn't a chance of that and he knew it.

"There's no lube out here," Simon added.

"I'll spit on my fucking hand." He realized how crass his words were and started to backtrack. He didn't want to screw this moment up. Simon wasn't used to being with a man. Not anymore. And even if he was, maybe that kind of thing didn't do it for him. He was a fucking heart surgeon who drove a Lexus and didn't watch TV. Maybe things like that turned him off. "I didn't—"

But Simon spitting in his own hand cut Trevor off. "Come here," Simon said, and he did. He obviously was okay with taking the lead now.

Trevor straddled Simon's lap as he sat on the couch. He was thick, really fucking thick, the head of his cock swollen and almost purple. Fat veins lined his shaft, and it was enough to almost make Trevor come right then.

Simon used both of his hands, wrapping them around their pricks, and started to stroke. Trevor thrust his hips forward, riding Simon's lap as Simon jacked them off together. He loved the way their cocks rubbed against each other. He watched Simon's eyes, looking for any sign that he was freaking out, but he wasn't. His look was a mixture of desire and concentration. It was almost as though he was performing surgery, the way he paid such close attention to what he was doing. To the way he held them and the way he worked them together.

"You have no idea how much I've wanted to do this." Trevor kept moving. "I felt guilty, so fucking guilty, but I couldn't help but want you."

He was surprised to see Simon erupt at that. Come pulsed from his slit, the first shot flying up between them, and the other running down his shaft, giving them another natural lube.

"Christ. I didn't mean that. I didn't mean to come so soon," Simon gasped. But he kept working them together, kept jacking Trevor off. "It feels so good."

It was those words that made Trevor let go, that made his own dick unload pulse after pulse of thick come, mixing with Simon's. Pooling in Simon's navel and drops mixing in with the trail of hair on his stomach.

"Finally," Trevor whispered as he climbed off Simon and onto the couch. He pulled Simon with him, who held back at first before he went easily, lying on his side, between Trevor's legs, his upper body half on Trevor's.

"The couch."

Trevor grabbed his shirt and wiped up their come. "All better."

"I'm exhausted."

"Go to sleep." Trevor noticed Simon massaging his right hand. He wanted to do it for him but knew it would upset him, so he only closed his eyes.

"The lights are on. So is the television." Simon tried to move but Trevor didn't let him.

"So? Go to sleep."

"Trevor…I…fuck, I just—"

"Shh. Go to sleep, Simon. Or if you want me to leave, tell me to. If not, then go to bed. I don't need your words, okay? It's not that I don't want them, but I don't need them. Not right this second." Because he knew how much Simon struggled with words. "There's time." Or at least, he hoped there was.

***

They didn't last long on the couch. Simon was surprised he slept at all. Not just because they were two men on a standard couch, but because he was sleeping with someone else. He hadn't actually *slept* with anyone except Heather.

Only an hour or two after they…what did he even call it? Had sex? Jerked off together? Simon was awake again.

"You think too much," Trevor's voice was scratchy. Simon didn't even realize he was awake.

"It's a bad habit. I spend more time thinking than I do anything else." He thought about his hand, and getting his career back more than he did anything about it. He thought and studied more than he had fun in college. He used his brain instead of his heart with Heather.

"You should do what I always did—try not to think at all. It's much more fun."

Simon sat up and rubbed a hand down his chest. It was sticky. From Trevor's dry come, he wondered? Trevor didn't move. He lay with his legs on either side of Simon, his dick flaccid in a bed of hair at his dark crotch. He didn't flinch when Simon took him in, studied him, though why would he? "Like I said, I've been with men before, but I always thought, even back then, that when it came to a committed relationship it would be with a woman." Maybe that's what made him freak out a little with Trevor. Because he knew that Trevor already meant something to him, even if it was only on a deep, friendship level.

He cursed himself silently when Trevor mumbled a, "fuck."

"I thought you didn't do this. Didn't talk about how you feel," Trevor added.

Simon didn't. Not normally. He wasn't sure if this counted as talking about how he felt, but he also needed to get this out. And it seemed that he said a lot of things to Trevor that he didn't say to most people. Things like, *I missed you.* "I don't. Not typically."

There was a pause, and then Trevor nodded once as though he got what Simon was saying. Simon talked to Trevor more than he did to most people. "Your um…friendship has come to mean a lot to me. I don't…I don't want to do anything to sacrifice that. But I can't…I don't know what this means, either. I'm not looking for anything serious. I'm still trying to figure out what I want to do with my life, now that I've lost the ability to operate and—"

Trevor interrupted him. "And I'm trying to figure out what to do with my life now that I actually have one. No one asked you for promises and declarations, Simon. We'll just take it as it comes. We'll be friends, and if we end up being friends who sleep together, we'll just run with that. We don't have to put a real name on anything or make commitments. I just know..." Trevor shrugged. "I know that even though I've been sober for over a year, I've felt like shit most of that time. There was a few weeks in there, when we were hanging out, that things weren't so bad. And then the last month, I felt like shit again. I'm not a thinker like you. It's probably why I fuck up so much, but it's just not who I am. I know I like spending time with you. That's enough for me."

Trevor was right. Why did Simon have to put so much thought into it? Why did he have to have all the answers? All he knew was he liked spending time with Trevor as well. He liked talking to him. That was enough for Simon too.

He leaned forward and covered Trevor's mouth with his own. Their tongues tangled, wrapped around each other as they kissed deeply.

Minutes later, half-hard but tired as hell, Simon pulled away and stood up. "I'm going to bed. I'm too old to sleep on this couch all night. Let's go." He held his hand out, his fucked up hand, and Trevor grabbed it, letting Simon lead him to his bedroom.

CHAPTER SEVENTEEN

Blake sat on the couch watching ESPN when Trevor came through the front door the next morning. His brother didn't speak as Trevor made himself a cup of coffee. He needed a shower. He had no doubt it was obvious what he spent his night doing. He smelled like sex, but he also knew the longer he let Blake fester, the worse their fight would be.

"Do you have my lecture prepared?" he asked, leaning against the table.

"Fuck you, Trev. I'm not your dad. I'm not here to lecture you." Blake was tense…stiff.

"But you do, don't you? You've been lecturing me for as long as I can remember. Lets have it so I can go get cleaned up."

Blake shoved to his feet. "I wouldn't have to lecture you if you didn't always screw up. Jesus, you're fucking him. This whole time you've been insisting he's straight and you're *fucking* him."

The urge to throw his coffee mug across the room hit. Before he did, he set it on the table. "For what it's worth, I thought he was straight until last night. And second, why do you care? Why the hell are you so interested in my sex life? I don't give a shit if you fuck Jason or some guy you meet in a club. Hell, fuck a woman and I wouldn't give you shit about that, either."

"Are you kidding me?" Blake tugged on his left ear. He did that when he was frustrated. "I couldn't care less about your sex life. Fuck who you want. Hell, I'm glad you're getting laid. What I care about is Rock Solid. What happens when you two break up? Or if you decide you're done with him without giving him any word. What happens if you start…?"

And that's what this was really about, wasn't it? It wasn't like they would be working with Simon for years or anything. It was a few months. This was about Blake's lack of trust in Trevor. He was scared that Trevor would start using again and screw things up for Rock Solid and their family. Maybe he thought Simon would hurt Trevor and he'd relapse. Whatever the reason, this came down to his fear that Trevor wouldn't stay sober.

He turned and fell into the chair. He rested his elbows on the table, forehead in his hands. His right leg bounced up and down with nervous energy as he tried to catch his breath. Trevor kept his eyes closed. Opening them wasn't an option because he couldn't handle seeing the doubt on his brother's face. "You have no reason to trust or believe in me. I know that. It fucking kills me, but I know it. Still… I *need* you to trust me, man. Not Mom, or Jason, or my sponsor. Not the people from meetings or anyone else. *You.* You're my brother. My twin. It's always been you and me. The only times it wasn't, those were my fault, and now I'm asking you to forget about that. I get it, but I'm asking anyway. I can't do this without you. I need you to believe in me."

They kept going around and around and things weren't changing, and that wasn't helping.

"Right now the only person in my world who I don't feel like I'm letting down is Simon. Again, that's because I didn't hurt him the way I did you, but…I can't lose that. Don't ask me to walk away. You have to trust that I know what I'm doing. That I'm not going to screw up. How can I do this without my twin?"

Trevor finally breathed when he felt Blake's hand on his shoulder. "Do you remember our twenty-first birthday? I wanted to go out with you so badly. You already had a problem. I think I realized that, but you were my big brother. I looked up to you, and you knew all these people in the city and places to go. I wanted to go out and get hammered with you that night. It's all I wanted. We were finally legal."

Trevor squeezed his eyes shut tighter, and tried to ignore the pain in his head, in his chest.

"You didn't show up and I was devastated. Jase was already twenty-one and he said he'd go out with me. He knew some gay clubs we could go to but I didn't want to. It was our birthday. You promised me and you weren't there."

Their twenty-first birthday? He could have sworn they spent that together.

"I stayed home all night. My mind wouldn't stop going. I was done with you. It didn't matter if we were twenty-one or not, if we were finally legal to go to clubs and drink, I didn't want anything to do with alcohol or you. You didn't come home until the next night. When you did, you didn't know what day it was. You thought it was our birthday, and then it was you who was so excited to go out with me. You missed our birthday and you didn't even know it…but there was the other part of you, who in your own way had come through for me that day. You left whoever it was to come spend your birthday with your brother. It didn't matter that I'd just sworn to myself that I wouldn't ever drink with you. All I could think of was the fact that you'd come through for me. It had been just as important to you to spend our birthday together, you were just too far gone to keep track of your days."

Trevor huffed, feeling every one of Blake's words in his chest. "Way to make a guy feel better." He meant it as a joke but neither of them laughed.

"I'm just trying to say, it might not be on your time schedule, but I'm trying to come through for you too, Trev. I'm trying, and I know I'm not the only one. Neither of us might not be able to do exactly what the other wants, when they want it, but we always come around. And no matter what, we're always brothers and we always have each other's backs."

Trevor kept his eyes on the table, but reached up and grabbed Blake's hand on his shoulder. They stayed like that for minutes, Blake standing next to Trevor, letting him know he was there. He might not always do it in the best way, but he was there. And Trevor letting him know that he was trying, too.

***

Simon sat on the couch, with his laptop on his lap. He'd been there for hours, looking up the same things he'd looked up a hundred times—hand trauma and surgery.

He read the same information a million times, some discrediting a new procedure and others praising it. It had been known to do great things, it said. Modern medicine was incredible. He couldn't do what he did and not believe that. In his years as a surgeon, Simon himself had performed what some people called miracles.

He didn't see it that way, though. He ran on logic, and logic told him a second surgery likely wouldn't change anything. The first surgery hadn't helped, nor had therapy. His hand just didn't have the same precision that it once did, and there was nothing he could do about it....but what if he could?

Simon's cell rang and he found himself smiling. He never had a problem being alone before. He'd preferred it. But it wasn't like that anymore. The house felt too quiet. He felt too quiet, and he wasn't sure how he felt about these new changes.

"Hello?"

"I think you had this whole thing planned...lure me in with your good looks and bad attitude. Make me miserable because I wanted you, and believed you were straight, and then just when I thought I was about to snap, you pounced. You got a sick pleasure from making me go out of my mind, didn't you?" It was Trevor.

"But you kissed me first. Doesn't that mean you're the one who pounced?" Simon held the phone with his left hand, his right one on his stomach, his thumb absently brushing back and forth. He was glad Trevor called.

"That's because I was out of my mind, remember?"

"Do you have any regrets?" Simon knew what the answer to that question would be. At least he hoped he did.

"Hell no!"

He chuckled. "Then stop complaining." Simon moved the computer from his lap and set it beside him.

"You?" Trevor asked after a pause.

He probably should but the answer came easily. "No." And then, "You sound off. Is everything okay?" Maybe that was something he wasn't supposed to notice but he did. There was a somber tone to Trevor's voice. He got it from time to time, but Simon was usually around him when he did—when he spoke about his past or something. This time, he didn't know, but he could hear it there.

"Listen to you, sounding like you know me or something." There was laughter in Trevor's voice but it didn't ring true.

"I know you." And Simon did. Maybe not in all the ways there were to know a person, but more than he'd known anyone in a long time. More than he wanted to know people. "Stop trying to make me talk. This is supposed to be about you."

"You never want things to be about you."

"So?" Simon replied.

Trevor sighed. "It's not a big deal. Blake and I got into it. It happens all the time. I love him, but he can be an ass when he wants to. He's worried about Rock Solid."

Simon didn't have to ask why to know the answer. "He has no reason to be. Regardless of anything else, you're doing good work. The two things are separate. Nothing outside of the remodel will affect it from my end." He meant that.

"I think he's more worried about me fucking it up than anything else."

"You won't." Simon wasn't a stupid man. He used his brain over everything else. There was no way he could be assured Trevor wouldn't slip, just like there was no way to know his hand would get busted up. Still, he said it.

"It's easier for you to say because you weren't around. You didn't see. I wasn't always a nice guy, Simon. You need to know that."

And Simon was? Maybe it was a different kind of trouble they'd been in, but neither had always done the right thing. Simon hadn't done the right thing by people in his life, either. "You won't," he said again. "You're lucky to have him. I know you know that, but just remember, it's because he cares." It was something Simon hadn't really had—family who cared.

"What about you? Do you have family out there to drive you bat shit crazy? I've never heard you talk about anyone other than Heather."

That's because he'd never had anyone. Not really. "No. My father passed away when I was eighteen. There was never anyone else." In a lot of ways, there hadn't even been him. Not in the ways that mattered.

"How did he die?" Trevor asked.

"His heart," came out automatically. And then, "I should go."

"Too much, huh? I get it. I'm not used to this, either. That's one thing I miss about being high all the time. I didn't have to worry about feeling things I didn't want to."

That made sense. Simon could understand that. And he also knew he wanted to see Trevor soon. "Monday. You can come over in the morning to run if you want."

"Hey," Trevor called out before Simon could hang up the phone. "You were right about one thing. You know me."

It was Trevor who ended the call first.

CHAPTER EIGHTEEN

Simon stood outside when Trevor got to his house Monday morning. It was early, still dark, as Simon leaned against the porch waiting.

"Am I late?" Trevor asked as he closed the door to his truck. He knew he wasn't, but it seemed like an easy thing to say.

"No. Come on." Simon nodded toward the driveway and the two of them fell into step easily as they made their way toward the road.

"I'm going to get this paved, I think." Simon's arm brushed against Trevor's as they turned onto the street.

"Of course you are. Wouldn't want a gravel driveway."

"Are you trying to say I'm pretentious?" Their breaths alternated; Simon in, Trevor out, Simon out, Trevor in, as their feet beat the asphalt in alternating steps. *Clop, clop, clop, clop.*

Trevor liked the way they were in-tune with each other, but not. It was as though they made a beat together, a song. "Maybe a little, but that's okay. I like you anyway." He nudged Simon's arm with his, and they continued the rest of their run in mostly silence.

When they got back to Simon's house, Trevor made a stop at his truck for his bag. They'd agreed that it made the most sense for Trevor to get ready at Simon's place on the days they ran together.

Trevor would be lying if he didn't admit that meant they'd also get to play together a little as well. Trevor had Simon and his body on his mind since the other night. It hadn't been enough. It made him feel…*real,* if that made any sense. As though he was getting a part of his life back, being with a man, enjoying himself. That's what Simon gave him—he made Trevor feel like *Trevor*, when he'd felt like a stranger for far too long. He wasn't only the recovering addict with Simon.

But then, spending time with Simon made him feel like a whole new person. His head was always clear, when it spent too many years being fucked up. It was a strange combination, feeling familiar, yet foreign in his own body. It didn't make sense that he felt like both things, but there you had it.

"Want to join me?" Trevor wagged his eyebrows at Simon as he hit the short hallway, on his way to the shower. "It would only be polite of me to thank you properly for the use of your shower."

Simon reached up and scratched his neck, avoiding eye contact with Trevor. "No…no, that's okay."

"Hey." Trevor took a step toward him. The unsure look Simon gave him didn't sit well with Trevor. He could let this go. Maybe he should, but that wasn't really Trevor's style. "We okay? There's no pressure here, you know?" His heart sped up, his pulse echoed in his ear. He'd been known to be a little too much for people. Trevor didn't know when to quit. It was why it had been so easy for him to become an addict. He didn't want to fuck this up. Didn't want Blake to be right about this.

Simon dropped his arm and looked at him. "We're fine. It's not you. I'm glad you're here. It's just a lot to take in. I'm not used to…"

He didn't get to find out what Simon wasn't used to. He could tell by the way Simon's words trailed off that he wouldn't be continuing. That was okay with Trevor, though, because he was glad to be here too. "I'm going to go. I hope you don't want to shower after me. I plan on using all your hot water."

He grinned when Simon laughed.

***

There were a lot of things Simon wasn't used to. Yes, he'd been with men before, but none of those guys had been people he cared about in any way. They'd been a way to let off steam, a night away from responsibility the same way Simon had been to them.

They'd been sex.

No matter which way he cut it, Trevor would be more because they were friends. Simon spent the majority of his time in denial about a lot of things, but not Trevor. They had a unique friendship. They gave each other something. It was apparent every time they were together. Even if it was just a reprieve from the loneliness. That is what made however things went forward with Trevor, if they moved forward at all, *different*.

He'd only ever had that with Heather and look how they turned out. Simon didn't know how to give himself to someone. He didn't know how to show that he cared. Not really. And maybe he put entirely too much thought into this, and all Trevor was looking for was a way to get off, but it was a lot for Simon to sort through.

Giving a shit about someone was a lot for him to deal with because he didn't do that in his personal life. He gave that to his patients. He gave them every drop of blood, sweat, heart, and his mind that he could. He wanted to save lives, but he'd never been able to give that to anyone outside of his career.

Getting involved with a friend put an extra layer of intimacy that Simon just wasn't sure how to deal with.

So he didn't. They continued to jog together in the mornings. They laughed and talked. Trevor used his shower before walking up the hill for work every day. Wrong or right, he wondered what the rest of Rock Solid thought. If they assumed he and Trevor were sleeping together or not, and he wasn't sure how he felt about that.

But then Friday rolled around, and the thought of spending the weekend alone made his chest ache. They hadn't talked about running. He wouldn't be able to walk up the hill and peek in on the remodel if he got bored.

He would be alone.

The way he'd always wanted.

What are you doing tonight? Do you want to come over? Simon stared at the text for a good five minutes before he hit send.

CHAPTER NINETEEN

"It's an adjustment, learning how to live again. Or maybe it's learning how to live for the first time. That's how it feels sometimes." Trevor shifted in his seat as he listened to the man speaking in front of the room. He kept shifting his weight from his right leg to his left, obviously uncomfortable. Trevor would feel the same way. Even watching him was awkward, because the words could be his own.

"How do you know the right way to do this? It's a struggle every day. There are some days I feel like I'm moving too quickly. As though I'm trying to get my life back before I'm ready, and what if that ends up hurting me? What if it makes me relapse? But then…it feels *good* really living. To experience my life in a different way than I let myself before."

Trevor leaned forward, soaking it in. Listening to his own thoughts being spoken from someone else as he held his coin in his hand. He loved the weight of it there. The reminder of what he was trying to do.

"That's what we're supposed to do, right? Learn to live? Really live? Be happy? Can you really rush that?" the man asked.

"What makes you happy?" another man questioned.

Rock Solid. Mom. Blake. Simon. Trevor answered the question even though it wasn't for him. Simon. That was a new one to add to his list. But it was true. Simon made him happy.

Trevor drove straight from his meeting to Simon's. It had been the plan since Simon texted him earlier in the day. It made for a rushed day—work, home for a quick shower, the meeting, and now Simon's. He had no idea what they were going to do, why Simon asked him over when the only time he'd seen Simon outside of work in the past week had been on their runs. Trevor considered stopping to ask if his friend wanted him to grab food before he got there, but he skipped the call and went straight over.

He felt an urgency beating through him. It was like a dull ache, starting beneath his skin and echoing out through his body.

What the fuck am I talking about? He laughed at himself, not really sure why in the fuck he felt so out of whack all of a sudden.

When he got to Simon's, Trevor clicked the lock on the truck and headed to the front door.

His fist just came down on the dark wood when Simon pulled it open. "Hey," Trevor managed to get out.

"Hi." Simon wore a pair of jeans and a button-down, short sleeve shirt. His left hand massaged the scar on his right one. His dark hair was messier than usual. His eyes were small, almost like they were narrowed, as though Simon never stopped scrutinizing the world.

He studied Trevor. In that moment, Trevor felt like he was the knowledge Simon was looking for, and he wanted the man to learn everything about him.

Maybe it was the biggest mistake he could make.

Maybe he was rushing it.

Maybe Simon would kick him out.

All Trevor knew was he wanted to live. He grabbed the front of Simon's shirt, pulled the man toward him, and took his mouth.

This was what he'd been waiting for.

***

Simon stumbled backward. Parted his lips and let Trevor inside. He smelled the hint of soap and cologne as he pushed the door closed, and then pulled Trevor closer.

"Tell me to stop." Trevor's mouth slid down his neck.

"Don't stop." The reply was automatic. He wanted this. Wanted Trevor. "I bought condoms."

Trevor laughed. "Me too. Means we won't run out."

They kissed their way to the bedroom. Simon's cock felt like it would erupt at any second. It ached with want. He groaned when Trevor's hand cupped him through his jeans, when he rubbed his palm against Simon's rod. "Shit." He grabbed Trevor's wrist. "You can't do that. Not yet. I want you this time." His experience would be a lot more limited than what Trevor was used to, but he knew what he liked. Knew what felt good to him.

"Have you?"

"You ask a lot of questions while you're having sex." Simon unbuttoned Trevor's pants, and then pulled the zipper down over his bulge.

Trevor pulled off his own shirt and tossed it on the floor. "It's a lot of pressure. You haven't been with a guy in, what? At least fifteen years. It's been mostly women for you. I just…"

"You're not going to fuck this up," Simon finished for him, because he knew that's what this was about. Trevor was scared he'd screw up.

There was a thank you in Trevor's eyes but he didn't speak it aloud. Instead he fell backward onto the bed, with his hands behind his head. "Good. Then come here and suck my dick."

A rush of desire shot through Simon. He wanted that. Wanted it so much he could hardly stand it.

Trevor lifted his hips when Simon pulled Trevor's pants and underwear down. He laid there, cocky grin, tattoos, piercings, muscled and tight-skinned. Christ, he was into a man younger than him with a nipple piercing. Simon suddenly wanted to nip it with his teeth.

Instead he let his eyes keep traveling to the path of hair from his navel to the thicker patch at his crotch with his long, swollen prick in the middle of it.

Heat skittered across his skin at the same time a shiver rocked through him. He was equal parts want and nerves. Trevor was right. It had been over fifteen years since Simon had touched another man, and he'd never wanted any of them as much as he wanted Trevor.

"Gimme your mouth, Simon." Trevor pulled one of his hands out from behind his head and held it out. "You want it. You want me. I see it. Tell me you want me, and then show me how much."

It was those words that shoved the nerves out of the way. He'd never had someone else talk to him like that, and it made his dick ache with need. Simon pushed Trevor's hand out of the way, went to kneel on the floor between Trevor's legs but ended up on the bed instead.

He lay horizontal to Trevor, his face right above Trevor's erection. "I want you. I want you so much, I can't get you the fuck out of my head." He didn't have any more words other than that. Now, it was only action. He'd show Trevor just how much he wanted him.

CHAPTER TWENTY

It was almost like he'd never had a blowjob before. Trevor wrapped a hand in Simon's hair as his hot, wet mouth took Trevor in. There was no deep throating. Simon didn't even try to take him to the back of his throat; just as much as Simon could handle, and it was enough to drive Trevor fucking crazy. "Fuck…yeah. Like that."

He looked down to watch Simon's head bob over him. Simon used his hand to pump Trevor's dick while he sucked him. He squeezed as his mouth went up and down, saliva making his hand glide easily.

"Christ, you're fucking killing me. So damned sexy. I've wanted you since the first time I saw you." Trevor used his hand to guide Simon, only slightly.

Simon tried to take him deeper, and gagged a little before pulling back and sucking him more shallowly again. Trevor didn't take his eyes off of him, even though they wanted to squint closed and shoot his load into Simon's mouth.

He felt over-sensitive. It had been a long time for him, but it was still early for the tightness in his balls to already be edging in. But then, in a lot of ways, this was all a first for Trevor too, wasn't it? There hadn't been a time in his life he hadn't at least been smoking weed when he was with someone. The first time he'd had sex, he'd been drunk and high. Later, as he drifted closer and closer to the edge, the alcohol was still there but there was also ecstasy, coke, or whatever else he could find.

But this time it was just Trevor and Simon, nothing else.

He wanted it to last forever. "My sac…I want your face there. Breathe me in, suck my balls." Maybe it was too much. Maybe it would turn Simon off, but…

His dick slipped out of Simon's mouth with a *pop,* and then his face was between Trevor's legs. He sucked Trevor's nuts into his mouth. Trevor moaned, slid a hand down Simon's back and palmed his ass. He wished like hell he'd taken the time to get Simon out of his clothes. He wanted skin. Wanted his fingers to trace the crack of Simon's ass. Wanted to fuck Simon with his fingers or his tongue.

"Come here." He grabbed Simon and pulled him up, parting Simon's lips with his tongue before fucking his mouth with it. Kissing him as deeply as he could, his hands in Simon's hair. His prick hurt, pulsed with a deep ache. The same ache that filled his whole body.

Trevor pulled his mouth from Simon's. "Take your clothes off. I want your cock. Fuck me before I can't wait and I end up fucking you."

***

Simon's dick jerked beneath his confining briefs. He wasn't sure if it was knowing he would have Trevor, or maybe even Trevor saying he might have Simon. That was something he hadn't done before, but saying he hadn't thought about it would be a lie. He wanted it.

Simon pushed off the bed, wishing like hell he hadn't worn a shirt with so many buttons as he undid them all. But then Trevor's hands were at his pants, taking care of those, shoving them down Simon's legs just as Simon finished with his shirt.

"You're going to have to spend some time getting me ready. It's been a long time." Trevor wrapped his hand around Simon's erection and stroked.

His heart skipped over a beat or two but then found its rhythm again. Trevor must have seen something in Simon's expression because then he asked, "Do you need me to do it? I'm ready for you. I made sure just in case."

"No." Simon shook his head. "I'm pretty sure it's like riding a bike." He tilted Trevor's head up and kissed him, owned his mouth as he pushed backward. Felt Trevor's lip piercing dig into his skin. Trevor moved, Simon crawling with him until Trevor lay with his head on the pillows, Simon leaning over him. Bent forward, and licked the bar in Trevor's nipple, then did it again. "I've been wanting to do that."

Trevor smiled.

And then Trevor rolled to his stomach, pushed his knees under himself with his ass in the air. Muscles flexed in his hairy thighs. Again, Simon's dick bobbed against his stomach. "I don't think I've ever been so hard." He wasn't exaggerating, either.

"Then get the fuck on the bike, Simon. Christ, I want you."

He loved Trevor's honesty. His hunger. It matched his own. Simon grabbed lube and a condom from the drawer before positioning himself behind Trevor. He kissed his way down Trevor's back. Stopped at the end of his spine, and thought about continuing on. That was something he hadn't done before, and he wasn't sure he was ready for it.

His hand shook a little as he lubed his fingers on his messed up hand. The hand that couldn't do what it was supposed to do anymore…but this? This it could.

He brushed a finger over Trevor's tight rim. Trevor's shiver rocked through to Simon, making him do the same thing. He rubbed it. Wanted to kiss it, but again, couldn't do that yet.

He felt Trevor tense up as he pushed the first finger inside.

"Fuck yes," Trevor hissed out. Simon didn't reply. Couldn't. He just watched his finger disappear inside Trevor's body. *In, out, in, out.* He played, fucked Trevor with one finger, then another.

"Jesus…that is so damn sexy, watching my fingers move inside you." Trevor started to move backward, his body meeting Simon's hand, when Simon spoke. "I'm probably going to come the second I get inside you."

Trevor laughed. "You'll make it up to me."

Simon scissored his fingers, stretched Trevor's asshole.

He worked a third finger in, watched him stretch as he listened to Trevor moan. Trevor grabbed his own erection and started to stroke. "Did I ever tell you I'm impatient? Get inside me."

Yes, he could definitely do that. Simon pulled his fingers free, ripped open the condom wrapper and rolled it on. He lubed himself, and Trevor. He was at Trevor's hole after that, his crown pushing into him.

His hands covered Trevor's ass cheeks, pulling them open as he watched his cock stretch Trevor and work it's way inside.

"Fuck. Fuck, fuck, fuck." Trevor's voice shook but there was nothing but pleasure in it. Simon felt it, too.

He couldn't hold back anymore. He didn't move in a quick thrust, but continued to ease his way inside until he was buried in Trevor's ass.

Trevor used one arm to lean on the bed as he bent with his ass there for Simon to take. His other hand worked his own cock, jacking himself off. Simon pulled out, then thrust forward again. Over and over he slammed into Trevor. The man's head hit the headboard but he didn't complain.

Simon's whole body felt tight, like a shaken up soda can ready to explode. Trevor's ass squeezed his dick, a tight fist pleasuring him.

He was bursting out of his skin, ready to implode, explode, and every other thing he could do. "So good… Trev…you feel so fucking good."

He pumped again, and that's when Trevor groaned, his ass tightening as he came. Simon couldn't hold back anymore. He didn't even try as he let loose, came apart, coming in wave after wave, filling the condom, sucking the energy out of him. He fell to the bed. Trevor collapsed, too, and Simon pulled the man to him, not giving a shit that he was leaking come all over the place.

He couldn't move, and didn't want to. He was pretty sure he could repeat this moment over and over and never get tired of it.

CHAPTER TWENTY-ONE

"How'd it start?" Trevor asked. "You with men. Did you always know you were bi?" He wasn't sure what made him ask. Maybe because it was such a surprise to him, being with Simon like this. Trevor never saw it coming before the other night.

It took Simon a minute to answer. "I'm not sure I ever really thought about it much. I've always kept to myself. It's just who I am, so I wasn't the guy dating my way through high school. College was different. It wasn't that I was that much more sociable. I just got horny." Simon laughed and Trevor felt it vibrate through the bed, to himself. Simon didn't laugh nearly enough. He decided to make it his goal to keep Simon laughing.

"Makes sense."

"I lost my virginity freshman year to a girl in a study group. Let me tell you, it was like an awakening in some ways. I sure as hell wondered what took me so long to do it." Simon pulled the condom off, tossed it in the trashcan and then rolled to his side. He leaned up on his elbow, looking down at Trevor, and he looked…relaxed. Relaxed in a way

Simon almost never let himself be. Trevor decided to keep that look on Simon's face too.

"So you started fucking women and…" He didn't want to be an ass, but that wasn't really what he cared about the most in all of this.

"Well, I don't want to make it sound like I was doing it every weekend. You have to remember, for me it was always about being a physician. That's all I cared about, but then, well, obviously sex felt good, and I needed to blow off a little steam every now and then."

"You were a slut," Trevor teased him. He had no doubts that Simon's past had nothing on his own. He shuddered to think about that.

"Do you want to hear this or not?"

Trevor was surprised when Simon reached over and brushed a thumb over Trevor's forehead. It was an intimate gesture, and not one Trevor was really used to with a lover. "Yeah. Keep talking. Get to the part where you were with men."

"Okay…the first time was a guy in my anatomy class. He was openly gay. I never gave it much thought, but I'd catch him looking at me from time to time. He had balls, I'll tell you that. He didn't know me from Adam but he didn't hide his interest. It didn't take me long before I realized I was watching him, as well. It was a surprise. I didn't know what to think of it, if I'm being honest."

"Let me guess, he asked you to study with him? I think I've seen this movie before. Have you seen the one where the construction worker nails the homeowner?"

Simon rolled his eyes, absently fingering Trevor's hair. "You keep interrupting me and I'm going to assume you don't want to hear this, but yes, he asked me to study. He went down on me. I protested for maybe…three seconds. I just remember thinking how sexy I found him. The difference in the way he touched me, the feel of his buzzed head against my thighs. I jerked him off afterward, and left telling myself it was a fluke. I was horny and he was there. But then it happened again. He asked me on a date afterward, and I made an excuse. He asked another day and I made an excuse then too."

Trevor shifted at that. It wasn't that he was lying here thinking he and Simon would ride off into the sunset together, and Simon did tell him that when it came to a lasting relationship, he always assumed it would be a woman. Still, it didn't sit right. "Because he was a man?"

"Umm…" Simon still fingered his hair. Trevor wondered if he realized he did it. "Maybe partially. I guess I would by lying if I didn't say that's partially what it was. I didn't really know what to make of it at the time. It wasn't only that, though. I just didn't have time in my life for anything other than spending a night here and there with someone. I had no interest in dating anyone, not only Andre. So, he moved on, I lost myself in school again, and the next time I was with someone…it happened to be another man. He was the first man I sucked off; you were the third, by the way, so there hasn't been a lot. The first guy I only jerked off."

"Holy shit." Trevor leaned up, resting his weight on his arm as well. Simon had only been with three men before him, hadn't fucked all of them, and had only blown two of them. "Three men? You're like a fucking saint." Trevor had never been a saint of anything.

"Hey, there were women in there, too. Don't make it sound like I'm virginal. But yes, there were only three men I've been intimate with before you. The third man I fucked, and then I met Heather. I hadn't been looking for anything serious with her, either, but it just happened."

This meant he'd only fucked one man before he met Trevor. Also, it didn't escape Trevor's attention that a relationship *just happened* with Heather when he didn't come close to it with any man. He felt his body go tight. He didn't have an excuse for it. Trevor knew that but it didn't change how he felt. "So the men were a way to get off until your princess arrived?"

He went to get out of bed but Simon grabbed his wrist. "Hey. Don't do that. That's not fair. I'm being honest with you here. Hell, I'm talking to you in a way I don't with anyone else. Who knows the why of it, Trev? Was it just that I was meant to fall in love with Heather? Maybe it could have been a man had I found the right one, but no, I wasn't getting off with a man while waiting on a woman. I was attracted to those men the same way I am to you. I knew who I was with when I had them, just as I know who I'm with now. If you're looking for me to have all the answers, you're going to be sorely disappointed. It's you who I want here with me. That's the only answer I have."

Fear pumped through him, mixing with his blood, filling his veins. Jesus, Simon meant something to him. Yeah, he'd know that before, but he realized then that Simon meant more to him than he'd let himself believe because he needed to hear that Simon wanted him here, when he'd never needed to hear that from any other lover he'd had.

"Shit." Trevor ran a hand through his hair before lying back down. "I didn't have a right to freak out like that." But he was. Inside he still was because he thought he might want more with Simon than just this. The timing sucked but it didn't change how Trevor felt.

***

There was a part of Simon that wanted to get out of the bed and walk away before he got himself into trouble. He didn't know if Trevor wanted answers. Simon only knew he didn't have them.

"I can't make you any promises." It wasn't because Trevor was a man…he didn't think. It was because he'd already fucked up spectacularly when it came to being in love, to having a relationship with someone, and that was before his hand got screwed up and he did nothing except feel sorry for himself. If he couldn't completely give himself to someone then, how could he now?

"I'm not asking for them. I'm not really in a place to give any, either. Hell, I'm still trying to keep myself sober everyday." Trevor smiled. It was that cocky, know-it-all smile he gave to the world. The one he used to hide the truth. He didn't want to add to that uncertainty, but he wasn't sure what else to do, either.

"I can tell you I don't regret this. I won't regret it if we do it again, and I can pretty much guarantee I want to. There was never a second that it bothered me you're a man. There was never a second I wished you weren't." That would have to be enough. It was all Simon had to give right now.

"It's because I'm so sexy. It's hard for most men to resist me."

Simon liked that, he realized. How Trevor lightened the mood when it got heavy, or how he made Simon smile. He'd never been the easiest person to make smile. People told him that too many times to count, yet Trevor was good at it.

Trevor lay on his back, Simon still leaning on his hand, his elbow on the bed, when he leaned forward and kissed Trevor's plump lips. His facial hair was rough against Simon's. His mouth and tongue demanding as it moved with Simon's. No, he definitely knew who he was with, and he liked it.

"Since you're so virginal, I can share something with you, too," Trevor said when they parted. "This, with you tonight, and the other night on the couch…I can tell you that they were the only sexual encounters I've ever had where I hadn't at least had a few drinks. You used sex as a break for studying while I used it to have fun and party."

Simon could hear it in Trevor's voice, the regret and pain. He spoke with it any time he mentioned his past. "You should be proud of yourself." Simon wondered if anyone had told him that. He wanted to make sure Trevor understood that he should be proud, and that Simon saw it. "It's not easy, what you're doing. Be proud. I respect the hell out of you."

"I'm trying."

When it came to being a doctor, Simon had a good bedside manner. He knew how to talk to people and what to say. He struggled with it more in his personal life, which was why, despite not knowing if this was something he should ask, he did anyway. "What happened to make you get clean?"

Trevor let out a deep breath, and then sat up. He leaned against the headboard. Simon didn't move, just lay there watching him.

"You don't have to tell me." But he wanted him to. For the first time in a long time, Simon cared about someone enough to want all of the pieces of who they were, and he wasn't sure what to do about that.

CHAPTER TWENTY-TWO

Trevor didn't know how to put this into words. How to organize all his thoughts in a way that made sense. A lot of the time, how he felt didn't even make sense to himself.

"I think it was coming for a while. It's hard to explain. Toward the end, I knew I had a problem. Before, I would deny it to myself. I hit a point where I knew, where some days I would think I was ready to get help, and then I'd go out on a bender again."

He paused again trying to sort through his thoughts. Trevor appreciated the fact that Simon stayed quiet, letting him do this in his own time and way.

"It was a night like any other night. We got some speedballs, mixed them with too much alcohol. I was out of my mind, fucked up. The whole night is only fragmented memories. I can tell you it felt like a good time when it happened."

It was always a good time, the best. It wasn't until afterward that Trevor had regrets.

"I don't know whose house we were at. It didn't matter. All we cared about was the drugs they had."

Thoughts bombarded him: the people he'd spent time with, the things he'd done. The packed bodies in the house. The people passed out everywhere. He hated himself in moments like these. When he thought about all the things he'd done.

"I remember leaving with a man. Fucking him in the car in some random alley in San Francisco." He winced at that part. None of what he'd done had been pretty. "I get checked every three months, just so you know." Because there had been not only a lot of sex in his past but IV drug use as well. "I can show you my latest test results, or go in again if you want. I probably should have thought about that before. I'm sorry." And he *would* supply results or get tested again if it made Simon more comfortable. He was pretty sure he'd always used a condom, but who in the hell knew?

"We're not talking about that right now. Go on." Simon's hand went to Trevor's thigh, resting there.

"Thank you… We did another speedball in the alley afterward. Jesus, I remember feeling like my heart was going to jump out of my chest. It's crazy, but I loved it. Loved that feeling. It was like I was invincible. We got into the car. Greg drove, not me. That's not an excuse, because he was just as fucked up as I was. Time must have passed, who knows how much. It could have been a full twenty-four hours. At some point, I passed out in the car. I woke up alone. We were parked at a house. I looked up just as Greg was walking toward the open door. Part of me wanted to go with him so fucking badly. It didn't matter how fucked up I was, I wanted more. We often went from one party house to another. I knew that had to be what he was doing. It's what we always did.

"But I felt like shit. My head definitely wasn't clear. I just wanted to get out, I needed air. I thought about taking the car. The dumbass left it running. Instead, I shut it off, stumbled out of the car and just started walking. It was stupid, getting out like that. We weren't in the city anymore, somewhere outside of it, only I didn't know where. But I just started walking. I wandered into the middle of nowhere, got lost, puked up my guts in the woods. I guess Greg didn't have much fun at the party because eventually he got in the car and drove away. I don't know where in the hell he was going because he was seventy miles away when he crossed the divider on the road and killed himself. He could have killed others too. I was passed out in the woods in my own vomit when he died."

Trevor's stomach cramped as he relived that day. Lying in his own vomit, in the middle of nowhere. The fact that the man he'd been with had died. The fact that Trevor very easily could have been with him. It would have broken his mom and Blake, losing him like that.

That day played through his head a million times since it happened—how Greg ended up finding out about a party out there. Why he didn't wake Trevor up to go in. There was no other option than going somewhere to get high, though. None that Trevor could think of. All he knew was that Greg had died and he narrowly escaped the same thing, not only by not going with Greg, but passing out the way he had.

"To some people maybe it wouldn't matter. He was just an addict. But I was just an addict too. I could have taken the keys. Could have kept him from driving in the first place. Could have gone into the party, or stayed in the car. Maybe any of those things could have saved him…he could have killed someone else! We both could have that day. What the fuck would I have done if we had killed someone?"

Trevor didn't realize a tear had slipped out of his eye until Simon wiped it. What the fuck was he doing? He didn't cry.

"So, yeah. He was just an addict, and maybe he wasn't even a good guy. But he died, and maybe I could have saved him. I didn't even know he died until the next day. I slept out there all night, and then had to call Blake to come get me. He told me on the way home. The next day, I left for rehab." He'd stayed clean ever since. Trevor wouldn't go back to living that way. He couldn't.

"It wasn't your fault—"

"Don't," Trevor cut him off. "Everything I did was my fault. I know that. There's no changing it. All I can do is try to make up for all the mistakes I've made and all the ways I've hurt the people I love—my mom, Blake, even Jason. He's been close to my brother so long, he's like family to me. I've hurt them all."

Simon's voice was soft, comforting, when he said, "You care enough to try and make it up to them. That's what matters."

He looked at Simon then, the stupid question filling his head. And…he just let it out. Didn't think of the consequences of asking or why he wanted to know. "You know who I have in my life that I care about. What about you? Who do you have?" Because really, he didn't know much about Simon other than the fact that he had an ex-wife, and all he cared about was being a surgeon.

"Heather," Simon didn't hesitate to say that. Then he paused, sat up and then pushed out of bed. “And you. There’s no one else. I wasn’t lying when I told you that. I’m going to take a shower.”

He was an asshole. He never should have asked that, because he knew it had upset Simon. “I need one, too,” was his reply.

Simon paused, then absently rubbed his hand. “Then I guess you better come with me.”

***

They showered together. Trevor gave him head when they got out, and then Simon ordered food. Pizza, again. They really needed to figure something else out, or make plans ahead of time so they had more options other than pizza delivery.

Simon’s bedroom was dark except for the laptop on his lap. He sat in a chair on the other side of the room. It was silent except for the sounds of Trevor sleeping—his breath whispering out, or his body moving against the sheets when he changed positions.

Simon didn’t know why he couldn’t sleep. He’d dozed for about two hours before he woke up and couldn’t get back to sleep again. He’d lain in bed a while with Trevor. He’d touched him, his arm, his tattoo, his shoulder, his neck and chest. Brushed his thumb over the nipple piercing, trying to figure out how they got here. How this felt different than the men he’d been with in college.

Why he felt like he needed it so much when he’d only ever needed surgery. As much of an asshole as it made him, he’d never needed Heather. He cared about her but he hadn’t *needed* her.

But he needed this.

That's what had prompted him to get out of bed. What made him go get his laptop, because that's all he did now—research, watch videos and study his craft as though it was something he would ever do again. Maybe other people with an injury like Simon's could still perform, but surgery wasn't your everyday career.

It was after an hour that he clicked his favorites and scrolled down to a link he'd visited a hundred times.

A new procedure for people with his nerve damage. It was controversial, but most things that mattered were. Most people didn't think it worked. How could it? But there was evidence to the contrary. And it made sense to Simon. In his field, nothing was completely black and white. He had performed what people thought were miracles. He'd fixed people who he didn't think he could fix.

What if there was a way he could be a surgeon again?

What if he couldn't?

That was the scariest part, trying and failing. For a man who hated to fail, where failing usually meant someone's life, sometimes it was easier not to try at all.

CHAPTER TWENTY-THREE

Things went on like that for a little over a month. They ran together a few mornings every week. On those days, if Trevor wasn't already at Simon's when he woke up, he made his way there, jogged and then got ready for work.

Trevor went to meetings twice a week. It was easy, he'd heard, to slow down when things got busy. Between work and Simon, things were pretty crazy for him, but he couldn't let himself lose that. He may not say it aloud, but he needed it.

His meetings helped keep him steady, because that was another thing he didn't mention aloud. There were cravings. There probably always would be. He just had to be strong enough to fight them.

At least a few days a week he stayed at Simon's. They fucked like crazy—on the couch, in the shower, wherever they could. There were some things Simon hadn't done yet, namely give himself to Trevor, but Trevor didn't push for it. That was something Simon hadn't ever done, and it wasn't as though he didn't enjoy Simon fucking him.

His brother made it obvious he didn't agree with how much time they spent together, but mostly he kept his mouth shut about it. Blake wanted to support Trevor. Trevor knew that. He just wasn't sure how.

Rather than going out, they stayed at Simon's the majority of the time. That didn't bother Trevor. He would rather it be that way. He always felt rubbed raw when he went into town. People had their memories of him, most of them not so good. Sometimes he was simply reminded of all the things he'd thrown away in his past. That was hard, too.

And there were people there he'd done a lot of partying with as well.

It was Friday, July 3rd. Trevor just finished his meeting and pulled into Simon's driveway when his phone rang. It was his mom. He hadn't talked to her much in the past month, so he knew he had no choice except to answer. "Hello?"

"Trevor Anthony Dixon, are you avoiding me? I've been trying to get ahold of you for two weeks!" Her tone was light, but he knew there was seriousness mixed in there.

"I'm sorry, Mom. It's been busy. We're working long hours at Simon's, trying to get it ready within the next four to six weeks. We have certain things we can't be late on, or it makes the contractors we hired out run behind as well. Between that, my meetings and—"

"And Simon. You can say it, you know. Your brother told me you're seeing him."

Trevor held in a groan and dropped his head against the seat. "It's not serious." Though he wasn't sure if that was true or not. It felt pretty serious to Trevor, even though they hadn't said so. It was maybe the only thing that had ever felt serious to him except for his sobriety.

"Still, I'd love to meet him. I've never..." She'd never met someone that Trevor dated before. Probably because he hadn't dated before. He'd partied and fucked. With Blake, at least she knew Jason. Family was important to her, and she always wanted them to know she supported them. But he also couldn't imagine asking Simon to meet his mother. It felt too serious, and Simon wasn't good with most people. He didn't have family of his own.

"What about the Fourth of July Fair? Maybe he can go with you when we meet up there."

Fuck. Trevor couldn't hold back his groan this time. He'd forgotten about the fair. Or maybe he'd tried to because he knew his mom would want him to go. It was a tradition. They'd gone since he and Blake learned to walk. It was also the first place Trevor had taken a drink of alcohol. Everyone in town went, including people he wouldn't want to see.

"You know what? Never mind. I don't want to push you, okay? I'll meet him when you're ready. Or I won't. You said it's not serious and I need to respect that. Whatever you want, Trevor, okay? If you don't want to go to the fair, that's all right too. Maybe we can have dinner sometime next week."

The truth was, he knew his mom was serious. The last thing she would want was to put pressure on him. It wasn't how she worked. And if she knew he was nervous about going to the fair, she would insist he stay home.

That's the part that killed him. He'd missed so much from the age of sixteen until now. He didn't do the things he used to with his mom or brother, and he wanted that back. Even if it wasn't for himself, but for his mom. He should be able to go to a carnival with her. What kind of man couldn't handle that? "Are you kidding me? Of course I'll be there. Maybe I'll even win you a teddy bear," he teased, and she laughed. It felt a whole hell of a lot better to make his mom laugh than it did to make her cry.

"Are you sure?" she asked, but he could hear how much it meant to her. There hadn't been enough happiness from Trevor to his mom, and he wanted to keep it there.

"Yeah, Mom, I'm sure. I don't think Simon will be able to make it, but nothing could keep me away."

***

Their evening was mostly quiet. Trevor was usually the one who started most of their conversations, and he hadn't said much. They watched a movie. It was Simon's turn to pick so it was a crime drama. The doctor did it, and Simon had been able to call it from the beginning. On Trevor's nights to pick it was usually a comedy or an old horror.

He didn't quite get the old horror thing. Or the comedies, really. Most of them were ridiculous, but Trevor seemed to like them. He liked Trevor, so it worked.

"I need a shower." Simon stood up and stretched, waiting for Trevor to come as well. He didn't usually miss the opportunity for a shower with Simon. "Are you coming?" he asked, eyebrows pulled together.

"Nah. I'm going to hang out here for a minute. I took one after work."

Simon frowned. Something was wrong. This was where he probably should ask Trevor what it was…but then, if he wanted to talk about it, he would. Simon knew he didn't like to be pushed so he just said, "Okay," and made his way to the bathroom.

He couldn't wait for the big house to be finished. He wanted his office and library. He wanted a bathroom where it wasn't a struggle to fit two men inside.

Two men… He pulled off his shirt and closed the door, thinking about how naturally those words had popped into his head. It was because he and Trevor were currently fucking. Who was to say they still would be when Simon moved into the other house? Yet, he'd just assumed. That wasn't something he typically did.

Simon's shower was quick. He wasn't one of those people who stood under the spray, soaking it in for minutes on end. Get in, wash up, get out.

He dried off and wrapped a towel around his waist. By the time he stepped out of the small bathroom the lights and television were off. He paused a minute. Did Trevor leave? He'd assumed he would stay, but then he noticed a soft light under the bedroom door.

Something was definitely wrong, and as much of an asshole as it made Simon, he almost turned and went for the living room. These weren't the things he was good at. Yes, he and Trevor talked a lot, but that was usually after sex, or it just happened organically.

It had always been a problem with him and Heather. He didn't understand her need for him to prod until she told him what was wrong.

You say it, or you hide it, that's the way Simon felt about it.

Still, he went for his room instead of the other part of the house. The lamp beside the bed was on, Trevor lying on his back, fully clothed with an arm slung over his eyes.

It wasn't the first time he took in how incredibly sexy Trevor was. His T-shirt rode up, showing tanned skin and hard muscles, dark hair that disappeared below his pants.

The tattoo that now got him hard, when before he saw them as mutilating your skin.

The goddamned piercing in his nipple that Simon liked licking.

His lips that Simon liked to kiss. His facial hair and how it felt against Simon's skin, and the stud in his lip too. Trevor's face held his youth, except a couple little lines by his eyes showing he obviously spent a lot of time squinting in the sun. He needed to wear sunglasses. He looked as young as he was, but it was his eyes that told a different story. His eyes spoke of all the things he had seen.

And suddenly, Simon wanted to take away some of what hid behind Trevor's closed eyelids. Wanted to take away whatever made him so distant tonight.

But he didn't ask. Instead he walked over, sat on the edge of the bed, and kissed Trevor's slightly-parted lips. It wasn't often that he initiated things. He was still finding his footing when it came to having what felt too similar to a relationship than what Simon should feel comfortable with, but right now, he wanted to give something to Trevor.

He grabbed onto Trevor's hair because he seemed to like that, and let his tongue dip into Trevor's opening mouth. Trevor returned the kiss instantly. He nipped at Trevor's lip, let his hand drift down Trevor's body, but then suddenly, Trevor rolled, pulling Simon with him. His towel came loose when he went.

Now on his knees, Trevor said, "Lie down."

"This is for you." Simon wanted to do something to make Trevor feel good, not the other way around.

"It will be," he replied. "Lie down. On your stomach." Trevor pressed down on Simon's back until he went. Then he was there, between Simon's legs, spreading them wide before doing the same to the cheeks of his ass.

He couldn't form a clear thought before… "Oh God…" This was new. This was incredible. Trevor's tongue brushed back and forth over his asshole. He should stop this. He wanted this to be about Trevor but…his tongue brushed Simon's hole again, little flicks back and forth before adding more pressure.

Simon pushed back into Trevor, then moved forward. Tongue on his ass, his cock thrusting against the bed. He knew people did this, of course. He'd thought about it himself, but he hadn't—not with the three men he'd been with, and none of them had done it to him. "Trev…"

"You like this, don't you? Wanted to do it for a while but didn't know if it would freak you out." And then his face was there again, buried between Simon's cheeks as he licked at him. Simon couldn't stop himself from fucking the bed, shoving his ass backward, wanting Trevor as close to him as he could get. Little jolts of pleasure shot through him each time Trevor's tongue brushed over him.

Trevor's tongue was suddenly gone. "You have such a sexy hole.

So tight and hungry for my tongue. I could spend all night eating you."

Simon looked back to see him stick a finger into his mouth, and then he tensed up as Trevor pushed it inside.

"Relax," was all Trevor said, and then it was a combination of tongue and finger, and the friction of the comforter against his erection.

Trevor's tongue moved faster. His finger pressed in deeper, touched Simon's prostate, and rubbed it.

The feeling was too much. Simon tried to hold it off, wanted this to last, wanted Trevor to come first, wanted a whole lot of things, but his dick had something else in mind.

He came in two long spurts, come on his stomach, the blanket, yet he still kept moving, Trevor still kept licking him. "All night," Trevor whispered. "My mouth and your ass."

Yes. He wanted that but, it wasn't all he wanted. As much as it killed him, Simon rolled over, grabbed Trevor to pull Trevor up to him, but he fought Simon. Pausing at Simon's stomach, he licked the semen there. Simon's prick jerked, still half hard. Christ, that was the sexiest thing he'd ever seen.

"I like eating every bit of you I can. Taste so fucking good," Trevor said.

Their eyes briefly caught before Trevor turned, something hiding in them. That's what made Simon reach for him again. Made Simon pull Trevor to him, hands on each side of his face. "What's wrong?" he asked. "You know I'm here. You can talk to me."

The words hadn't been quite as hard as he thought they would be.

CHAPTER TWENTY-FOUR

Well, now he felt like an idiot. He'd been down all night. It happened that way sometimes—a hard time at a meeting, or cravings that were strong. When the memories bore down on him too much, or he looked at his mom and saw the pain there.

Sometimes it happened without a reason, and he didn't even realize it. But tonight, he'd known he was keeping to himself. Now, it felt so small. "It's nothing, really. There's the Fourth of July carnival tomorrow. My mom wants me to go. It's something we've always done as a family. It's just…" he pulled back, making Simon's hands fall away and then lie beside him. "Everything feels different now. Every part of my life. This fair, it's tied into my past, and I'm struggling to figure out how I feel about that."

"And you're scared it will make you want to fall back into old habits?" Simon asked.

Trevor wasn't sure how Simon knew that. "Everything I do, every single day, makes me scared of falling back into old habits. That hasn't gone away yet. I'm not sure if it ever will. But this? Yeah, it's like that everyday feeling times a hundred. And it shouldn't be. I hate that it is. I should be able to do this for her without that fear. I *want* to be able to do it for her without that fear." It made him feel weak. Like that guy who woke up in the woods in his own vomit.

"I would think that's normal, Trev—"

"I like that. When you call me Trev." He probably shouldn't admit that but it was true.

Simon didn't respond to what Trevor said, only continued his previous sentence. "It's normal to feel that way. There are some forms of healthy fear. You can do it. The fact that you're thinking about it so much proves it. And..." he paused for a second, touching Trevor's hair. "I know it's not much. I'm not sure what I could do, but if you want, I'll go with you."

That was a big-ass offer from Simon. Trevor felt it in the tightness in Simon's body, and the strain in his voice. Even without those things, Trevor would know it, because, "My mom will be there. My brother too. That means you'll be meeting her. She *wants* to meet you because she knows we've been spending time together." Simon obviously knew his mom would be there, but he had to be sure Simon really got it.

It was a big step, meeting the family, even if Trevor only introduced him as a friend (which was what he would do).

"I know," was all Simon said. Then he stripped Trevor out of his clothes, jerked him off, and said, "Turn out the light."

Trevor did, before they rolled on their sides, away from each other, and went to sleep.

***

Simon's stomach was in knots as he got out of his car. Trevor had already stepped out of the passenger side, and stood there waiting for him.

He'd told Trevor he would do this.

Part of him wanted to do this.

The other part didn't know how.

He'd never felt comfortable with Heather's family. Not in the way a family should. He spoke to her father, doctor to doctor. They spent holidays with them, and every one of them was spent with Simon tense. This wasn't something he really knew how to do.

"You okay?" Trevor asked, his brows pulled together as they so often were.

"Yes." Only he wasn't sure he was. How could he do this? Give part of himself to Trevor? Meet family, laugh, smile and pretend he was the kind of man who knew how to really be intimate with someone?

And they were doing it in public. Would people know that Simon and Trevor were together? Did he care about that? In college it had been about sex, and nothing more. It had all been behind closed doors, but this was different.

"If you don't want to do this, don't. I'll be fine. I don't need you here holding my hand." Trevor's voice sounded as cut-off as Simon felt. Did he not want Simon here either? If neither of them thought they were ready for this, maybe that would work better.

"I—"

"Trevor!" a woman's voice cut Simon's off. They looked at each other, both realizing it was too late.

Simon's eyes darted up to see a woman who…didn't look much older than he was. She had dark hair like Trevor did, hers long and hanging halfway down her back, tied back in a ponytail. He noticed strands of gray here and there, but that was the only indication of her age. She dressed simply in a pair of jeans and a button-down shirt.

Jesus. What were they doing? He could just as easily be here with Trevor's mom as he was with Trevor. Probably more easily.

He wasn't sure why he'd imagined Trevor's mom older—maybe the fact that she hadn't remarried; but the closer she got, the more it was obvious that she had to be under fifty.

Blake stood beside her. He gave Simon a tight smile as she reached out and hugged Trevor. "Hey you," she said.

"Hey, Mom." Trevor pulled back. "This is my friend Simon. Simon, this is my mom, Tiffany."

Her eyebrows pulled together the same way Trevor's often did. Was it his age, he wondered? Was she as surprised as he was that they could very likely be closer in age than Simon and Trevor were? It ate at him, knowing how young Trevor was. Would she think Simon was taking advantage of him? That Simon was too old for him? Did he care?

"Hi, Simon. It's so nice to meet you." Simon froze up as she pulled him into a hug the same way she had Trevor. No, this definitely wasn't him. He didn't do this. He sure as hell never hugged his own father, and he remembered hugging Heather's mom one time—on their wedding day.

"It's nice to meet you as well." Simon heard the stiffness in his own voice.

"Let go of the man, would ya? You're acting like I introduced you to my future husband." Trevor obviously meant the words to break up the tension, but all they did was made it thicker.

Simon rubbed his right hand when Tiffany stepped backward. "I'm sorry. I've never met one of your boyfriends before. I got a little excited. A mom is entitled."

Boyfriend. Simon closed his eyes, pulling in a deep breath. He was a boyfriend. He'd only ever been that to Heather…and now, on top of it all, he suddenly had a boyfriend of his own.

What the hell had he been thinking doing this?

CHAPTER TWENTY-FIVE

Trevor felt like he was in a box, an invisible box that no one else could see, yet he couldn't get out of it. It moved with him, getting smaller and smaller as he walked and talked with people. As he said hi to friends of his mom's, the owner of the beauty shop that he'd busted out a window in when he'd been twenty-one and drunk. His math teacher who caught him smoking marijuana behind the gym his senior year. They all looked at him and smiled, yet he felt the disdain.

They knew a lot of his stories.

They'd seen the pain he put his mom and Blake through.

They had every right to look at him as though they didn't trust him. Each of them that he passed, each of them who gave him a fake smile, sucked more and more air out of the invisible box surrounding him.

"So, how long have you been in town, Simon?" his mom asked.

Simon walked next to Trevor, on the far end of the group, a good two feet away from him. "Not long. It's only been a couple months." He didn't offer anything other than that.

“Are you from the area?” His mom tried to keep the conversation going as they worked their way through the crowds starting to fill out around them.

“No. I went to college back East and then moved out here for medical school with my wife. Her family is here.”

Trevor’s mom stumbled, and Trevor held in his groan. They really hadn’t thought any of this through.

“Oh…I didn’t realize you were married…” she replied. He heard the question in her voice.

“He’s divorced. It’s not important. Look, Mom, there’s the baseball booth. I promised to win you a bear. Let’s go.”

He could tell Simon tried to ease himself into the conversation when he said, “No one wins these things.”

“Trevor will.” His mom beamed at Simon.

Blake added, “He was the best pitcher this area has seen. He played varsity our freshman year in high school. We won state that year.”

“Blake.” Trevor tried to get him to quit speaking. Either he didn’t get the message, or he was ignoring it.

“He quit after that. Didn’t play again. Probably could have gotten a scholarship if he’d kept at it.” They all knew what Blake meant by that. Trevor had gotten into other things, he’d lost track of what was important and fucked up his life. “Oh, I see Jason up there. I’ll be back in a minute.”

Blake walked away. His mom shook her head as though she didn’t know what to do, and Simon stood in the background, without a word or a look in Trevor's direction.

The box got tighter around Trevor, and the voice he mostly kept quiet in his head got louder… *This would all be a lot easier with a drink...*

***

Simon watched as Trevor threw a baseball over a hundred miles per hour. It hit the target, knocking down all the jugs. He did it two more times. Three for three, and won a stuffed animal for his mom.

Simon hadn't known that Trevor played ball. That he'd lost a possible future in it. That struck him deeply for some reason.

As Tiffany stood picking out what animal she wanted, something made Simon reach out for Trevor. His hand hardly brushed Trevor's arm when they both pulled back at the same time. "Trev…" he started, but didn't go any farther. He knew Trevor felt like shit. Knew that his brother had upset him. That the whole evening was hard on him, yet he didn't say anything else.

"Drop it. It's no big deal," was Trevor's reply before he joined his mom. Once she got her oversized elephant, they started walking again. They didn't make it but a few feet before Trevor pointed to a picnic table. "Why don't you guys wait there? I'm going to hit the bathroom real quick."

"Trevor," his mom started but Trevor cut her off.

"I'm going to the bathroom, Mom. I'm a big boy. I won't get lost."

He walked away without a word to Simon. He wasn't sure what to do besides follow her to the table where they both sat.

She fidgeted, looking nervous. "Do you not trust him?" Simon asked.

Tiffany looked up at him, surprised at first, maybe because he was initiating a conversation, or maybe because it clued her in to the fact that he knew about Trevor's past.

"It's automatic sometimes. I know I need to have more faith in him. He's right. He's only going to the bathroom, but I worry about him so much. He's my son. I love him."

Simon scratched the back of his neck. How did he do this? Have a heart-to-heart with Trevor's mom about him?

"He understands. He's doing well, though. You should be proud." The words came out in an awkward rush, but they seemed to be the right ones since she smiled.

"Thank you. That's good to hear. When he's with Blake, I know he's okay. No offense, but I don't really know you and—"

"None taken. I understand what Trevor is going through, and I wouldn't do anything to make that journey harder on him."

She paused for a moment, and Simon could tell she had something else on her mind. He really wished Trevor would hurry and get back. Hell, he would be satisfied with Blake at this minute. He would rather gnaw off his own arm than hear what she had to say.

"There's never been anyone he cared enough about to introduce to me before. I know it was my idea, but he still did it. I just…he would kill me for saying this. I know he's a grown man but he's still my son, and he's going through a lot. I don't want him to get hurt."

And she worried Simon could hurt Trevor. That was probably very likely. He'd done it before. "We agree on that." It felt like a hand was around Simon's throat. Like his breaths were getting harder to come by. He had the ability to hurt Trevor. He knew he did. Christ, the man had enough to worry about, enough going on in his life. Now wasn't the time to add Simon to the mix. Especially when Simon likely couldn't give Trevor what he deserved. He couldn't navigate a real relationship with his wife. How could he handle not only his first real relationship with a man, but with a man working on his sobriety?

"Can I ask if you're serious about him? You have an ex-wife…I have to admit, that's a surprise to me. Do you have kids? I just never saw Trevor with someone at this point in his life who is so…settled."

Simon leaned his elbows on the table. He was a thirty-seven year old man. Talking about his relationship with the parent of his lover wasn't something he felt he should have to do. Maybe that was because he didn't really like to talk to anyone about much, or maybe it was because he wasn't sure how to answer. He understood her worry and concern for her son, but he couldn't talk to her about this, either.

"You know what? Never mind. I have no right to ask you that. You mentioned medical school earlier. So you're a doctor?"

Of course she would bring up the other thing he didn't want to talk about. Though, did he really want to talk about anything? "I was a surgeon, yes. My hand was injured so I can't operate anymore." He glanced up but still didn't see Trevor coming. "I'm sorry to cut this evening short, but I'm really not feeling the best. I think I need to head home. Can Trevor get a ride home with you?"

Her eyes went wide and he noticed they looked exactly like

Trevor's. "Um…yes…sure."

"Please tell him I'll call him tomorrow." Without another word, Simon got up and walked away.

CHAPTER TWENTY-SIX

Trevor knew the second he walked back into the crowd of people and saw his mom sitting at the table alone that Simon had gone home. He'd expected as much when he went to the bathroom. He'd given him enough time to make his escape, figuring it was probably easier on them all.

It was stupid to have Simon come here with them tonight. But knowing Simon would leave and trying to make it easier on him to do it still didn't stop the anger from bursting through Trevor when he saw that Simon was actually gone.

He'd thought it was best, but now it pissed him off. Simon knew Trevor was nervous about being here tonight, and he just left. But then…it wasn't Simon's job to be whatever Trevor needed, either. It was a fair for Christ's sake. If he couldn't handle this, how could he handle life?

"Simon wasn't feeling well. He asked me to tell you that he'd call you tomorrow," his mom said when Trevor joined her at the able.

"Yeah, he wasn't feeling well earlier," he lied, having no doubt his mom knew exactly what he was doing.

"I think it was partially my fault. I was surprised that he'd been married to a woman. And that he's a bit older than you."

Trevor shook his head. "People are bisexual. It happens. And he's thirty-seven, it's not a big deal. I feel older than that every day of my life."

She cocked her head at that. "You do?" He could hear the sadness in her voice. It was the last sound Trevor wanted to hear.

"I'm fine, Mom. I've just lived too much life for a twenty-five year old. And I told you, it's nothing serious. We're friends."

"He's quiet. I didn't get a good read on him."

"I'm quiet now too…and he's not always that way." The need to defend Simon came automatically, despite the fact that he was pissed at him.

She didn't look at Trevor when she said, "He means something to you. I see it, even if you don't. I'm happy for you but scared at the same time. I just worry it's not the best time for you…"

Those words were like a kick to the stomach. Each syllable another sharp pain piercing Trevor. They had no faith in him.

"I know what I'm doing." Though he didn't. Trevor rarely did. "I think I need to go." He stood and his mom nodded. They hugged before he told her to call Blake to come and meet her at the table. "Tell him I took his truck, okay?" Trevor had keys to it. Blake would probably be pissed, but right now Trevor didn't care. He could ride home with their mom or Jason.

He'd just made it out of the gate when the fireworks started, reds, greens and golds lighting up the sky. He stopped to look at them. He'd always loved the fireworks. It had been his favorite holiday as a kid.

"Trevor? Holy shit, is that you? I'm sure as hell hoping it is, because if it's Blake, you're probably going to kick my ass."

Trevor froze at the voice talking to him. Obviously, it was him since Blake didn't have any of the piercings that he did.

"It is you! Hey, man? What's up?" It was another male voice he recognized. Paul and David. He'd partied with these two men more times than he could count. His stomach twisted in knots at the same time that he wanted to step closer to them. He wouldn't be surprised if they didn't have something to drink on them right now. No one was watching. If he slipped away with them, his family would never know. And after the night he'd had, Trevor deserved that.

No. He couldn't do that. Wouldn't. "I'm just heading out. Maybe I can catch up with you guys another time." His voice sounded strong. Trevor was proud of that.

"You want to leave with us? We were thinking of hitting up the Homestead," Paul asked. It was one of the local bars in Rockford Falls.

Do it.

Don't.

No one would know.

I would.

Trevor's thoughts warred with each other. "I really can't."

"One drink won't hurt. It's been too long." This from David.

It's only one drink...

His brother was already pissed at him anyway. He'd already hurt his mom. Simon left. What could it hurt?

That's when he felt it...the cool glass bottle in his hand. The liquid on his tongue. The burn of it sliding down his throat. He missed it. Missed it so fucking much sometimes—the feeling of being numb. He closed his eyes, imagining the tingle move through him that would dull into a numbness. He could do this. He could go.

But then, he saw his mom...Blake...Simon. He saw his own face in the mirror and thought about the hate for himself he would see reflected there if he went with them.

Trevor shook his head. "No. I can't. I don't drink anymore." Never again. He went to walk away but Paul grabbed his arm.

"Come on, man. You're being rude." Paul didn't let go.

"You act like we didn't used to be friends. Hell, we haven't even seen you since you've been back." David said.

The pull teased him again. Trevor wanted to go. After all this time, he wanted to go.

But he wouldn't. He jerked his arm away.

"That's fine. You always were a dickhead. You started that business with your brother and now you think you're better than the rest of us? Fuck you, Dixon." David shoved him. They were close enough to Trevor now that he could smell the alcohol on them.

It went right to his head, and he followed his first instinct. He swung. His fist connected with the side of David's face.

He shouldn't have done that. He'd known the second he did it. It was his lack of impulse control, but he didn't have much time to think about it after that. Paul punched him in the face, then David in the stomach. Pain shot through both areas.

Trevor swung again, connecting with someone or something, then another fist hit him right before, "Hey! What's going on over there?" someone yelled.

Paul and David ran off.

"Hey! What do you think you're doing?" The voice came again. Trevor could feel his lip bleeding. Feel his eye swelling.

He knew this would end fucked up. And somehow, it would be his fault. "I'm fine," he called before heading for the parking lot, getting into Blake's truck and driving away.

***

Simon's phone rang not long after he got to his house. His first thought was that it would be Trevor, but with a glance at the screen, he realized it wasn't. "What?" he snapped at his ex-wife. It wasn't until that second that he realized he *wanted* it to be Trevor. He felt like an ass for leaving the way he had. He didn't want to fight with Trevor. He deserved better than the way Simon had treated him tonight.

"Whoa. You haven't sounded like that much of an asshole in at least a month. What's going on?"

Talking to his ex-wife about this was not on his list of things he wanted to do. "Nothing."

"You sound like a child. Geez, Simon. It doesn't hurt to talk to someone. And even if you don't want to, you can at least act like a grown man about it."

She was right. He knew that.

"Come on. I'm happily planning a wedding. I need some drama to make up for all the happy we have over here."

He couldn't help but chuckle. "Thanks for counting on me for the bad..." He took a deep breath, and then, "I was an ass. I went with Trevor to a local fair. It was...awkward to say the least. I was meeting his mother for the first time. I'm pretty sure I gave off the worst first impression possible before leaving while he was in the bathroom."

The other end of the line was silent so long Simon thought they'd been disconnected. Finally, Heather spoke. "Tell me if I'm way off base here, Simon. I'm sure I am but, I have to admit, it sounds like you have something more than friendship with this man."

Shit. He sat in a chair at the table. He hadn't thought, just spoken. Of course what he said would make it obvious. And the truth was, Heather didn't know Simon had ever been with men before. "Would it matter?" he finally asked.

Another pause. "You know me better than that. Of course it wouldn't, but I have to admit I'm shocked. Is that...have you always been gay? Is that why it didn't work with us?" There were more questions...pain and more questions in her voice. She had the right to feel those things.

"I'm not gay, sweetheart. I'm using bisexual, I guess. I've never labeled it before. I had...before you...but I'm not gay. I was attracted to you. I wanted you. I did love you, Heather."

He heard her sniff and knew she was crying. "I'm not sure if knowing that helps or not. Maybe it would be easier to say my marriage failed because you're gay. That way I could blame it on you."

Because she couldn't already? "We both know I was responsible no matter my label. The same way I'm responsible for tonight." Trevor had needed him. When did Trevor really ask for anything? He'd needed Simon and Simon failed him.

"I don't know." Simon shook his head. "I don't know what to do."

There was a shaky intake of breath through the line. "He means something to you…more than I did."

He wasn't sure how to respond to that so he didn't.

"Don't walk away. Apologize. You may not think you can do it, but you can. Fix it, Simon. You deserve love too." She'd also told him that the last time he saw her. He couldn't say this was love. He didn't want to think about whether it was or not. That just made things more difficult. But the truth was, he hated that he let Trevor down. Hated that he walked away from him and that they were fighting. He wanted to fix it. He wanted Trevor here with him.

"I don't know how."

There was a pause before Heather said, "For such a smart man, you sure can be stupid. You'll figure it out, Simon. I know you will."

CHAPTER TWENTY-SEVEN

Trevor was lying on the couch with a frozen bag of peas on his eye when the front door opened. He should have gone to his room, because there was only one thing that would happen when Blake saw him. Hell, maybe he wanted that. Maybe he was itching for another fight.

"Ah, shit, Trev. What did you do?"

In his brother's defense, he'd seen Trevor black and blue from too many fights to count. If he was drunk or high and someone pissed him off, they came to blows. It was just the way things were, but that didn't mean it didn't sting that Blake's first instinct was that Trevor had fucked up. "Screwed up. What else?" And then there was the obvious, he had swung first.

Trevor sat up and his head spun. Shit, they'd knocked him a good one. Pain pulsed through his head in powerful waves.

"Fuck." Blake ran a hand through his hair and Trevor almost laughed. It wasn't something his brother did any time other than when he was stressed about Trevor. "What are you on and who did you fight with? Do you remember? Are they okay?" Blake paced the room, nervous energy bouncing off of him.

It wasn't fair of Trevor, but as each second passed by he got angrier and angrier at his brother. He was supposed to be there for Trevor. He shoved to his feet, dizziness hitting him again. "You know what? Fuck you, man." He didn't even ask if Trevor was okay. His only worry where Trevor was concerned was what he took.

"Hey." Blake grabbed his arm. "Where are you going? We need to get you to rehab and I need to know what happened with the fight."

The whole night came back to Trevor in flashes—Simon being uncomfortable, Simon leaving, the alcohol…fuck, he'd wanted to go for that drink so bad. Didn't Blake get how hard this was for him? How much work it was? His head spun again. Every fucking day was a challenge, yet he was doing it. Couldn't he get some credit for that?

"They're fine."

Blake winced.

Trevor pulled his arm free and dropped the frozen peas to the coffee table. "That's right, there were two of them, against me. No worries. I'm sure I got the worst end of it. They ran off before I did."

Trevor took a wobbly step before snatching his keys off the kitchen table. "They were people I used to party with. They wanted me to party with them tonight. I said no, they were assholes about it."

Trevor made it to the door before Blake spoke again. "Why didn't you say something? You said you screwed up. I just thought…"

"Because for once I want you to have a little bit of faith in me. For once, have my fucking back because you're my brother and you trust me.

With my past, it's a selfish thing for me to want. I get that. But we both know I've always been good at being selfish."

Trevor slammed the door on his way out. He heard it open again and Blake shout his name but Trevor ignored him. When he closed his truck door, it felt like he had hit his head with it, his brain hurt so badly.

He didn't drive far before he knew he had no business behind the wheel. His head and face ached too much for it. Trevor made a quick turn into the park. Being the farthest he could from the road made the most sense so Trevor headed for a spot at the end of the lot. There was a small corner with a few parking spots hidden from the road so he chose one of them. He laid his seat back before killing the engine.

He could go to his mom's, but he didn't want to be around people right now. A hotel room was too far away.

Automatically his eyes closed, and he wished he'd brought the peas with him for his face.

When did this get easier? The urges and the cravings. His family. When did he earn their trust back? He'd done what he was supposed to tonight. He'd been there for his mom, and then said no when he could have easily fallen off the wagon.

But he hadn't. He'd done the right thing, and yet he was still sleeping in his truck the way he'd done too many times to count when he'd been fucked up.

What the hell was the purpose in it all if he still felt like a screw up no matter what he did?

***

Simon didn't sleep all night. He replayed his phone call with Heather over and over in his head. Just from the sound of his voice, she'd known Trevor meant something to him…and he did. Trevor really meant something to him.

He helped Simon forget about his hand. Made him laugh, made him feel good. When was the last time he'd really felt good about anything other than his work? Even before his injury, it had always been about being a surgeon and nothing else.

There had never been a time in his life where he felt like he was, or could be, more than Dr. Simon Malone, surgeon. As much as he'd loved Heather, he'd never felt like more than Dr. Malone with her. He sure as hell never felt like anyone growing up. Yet he did with Trevor and he didn't understand why.

But he knew he wasn't ready to give that up yet.

It was early, about seven, when Simon called Trevor. It went straight to voicemail. He tried again but got the same thing. He deserved it. There was no question about that. He'd been an ass last night. He was an ass often.

He shoved out of bed and pulled on a pair of jeans and a T-shirt. Simon grabbed his keys and went for the door. If Trevor wasn't going to answer his phone then he'd have to deal with Simon in person.

Halfway to Trevor's his phone rang. He answered, and before he could say hello, Trevor spoke in a sleep-laced, scratchy voice. "You ran away."

"I did. I'm coming to you right now if that helps."

There was a moan through the line. It didn't sound like it was only from lack of sleep. “What’s wrong?” Simon kept his phone between his shoulder and ear, eyes on the road.

“Nothing a little rest won’t help. I got into a fight with two men after you left. I’m a little out of practice, and then—”

“Are you okay?” Guilt and fear made Simon’s foot push heavier on the gas pedal. Christ, he’d left Trevor and he’d gotten into a fight?

“You asked if I’m okay…” Trevor sounded amazed.

“Why wouldn’t I?”

There was a pause and then, “They were old friends, if you can call them that. They wanted to party, but I didn’t. I—”

“I know. I trust you. That’s not what I’m worried about. How bad is it? I’m almost to your house.” He should have been there for Trevor. In this moment, Simon couldn’t even remember why he’d left. Trevor was always there for him. He was his friend, and his lover. Simon had left when Trevor needed him.

Trevor laughed humorlessly. “Not home. I got into an argument with Blake. Slept in my truck.”

Simon cursed. He got it. He hadn’t been there to experience the things Trevor had done. He’d never hurt Simon. He’d never lied to him, but still he saw red that Trevor’s brother struggled so much to support him.

“I can come to your place.” Trevor groaned again.

“No. Where are you? I’d rather check you out before you drive.”

“Because you want to make sure I really wasn’t drinking.” It wasn’t a question. He obviously believed that to be true.

And it wasn't. Maybe it was naïve of Simon to believe in Trevor but he did. "No. Because I need to make sure you don't have a concussion or something."

Trevor took a few breaths before replying. "There's a park just up the road from our house. I'm hidden at the back of the lot. Really, I'm fine, Dr. Malone."

The name made him smile. A month ago, it wouldn't have. "I'd rather be sure." They were both quiet for a second before, "I'm sorry. I shouldn't have left. I just…" He just what? Was weak? Scared? All of the above?

"I know. Me too," Trevor replied, knowing what Simon meant without him having to say it.

"But you wouldn't have left."

"Don't compare your sins to mine. I'll beat you every time. Come get me, Simon. We can figure out the other shit later."

He wanted to, he realized. He didn't want to walk away. For the first time, Simon wanted to do whatever he could to fix whatever was broken in his relationship with another person.

CHAPTER TWENTY-EIGHT

Trevor hadn't slept for shit the night before, so it was the first thing on his agenda when he got to Simon's. That was after Simon tried to decide if he had a concussion or not. He hadn't wanted Trevor to drive either, so Trevor had texted Blake (who'd called numerous times throughout the night) to tell him he would be at Simon's, and asked him to get Trevor's truck.

His brother had replied with "yes" and "I'm sorry," but Trevor still needed to figure out what he wanted to say to him.

And then, he'd slept. Simon gave him some Tylenol and he spent the rest of the day in Simon's bed.

It was early evening when he climbed out. A note sat on the bedside table telling him that Simon had gone to get them dinner. You wouldn't think it could be that hard to cook a good meal. Simon performed surgery and Trevor could build a house, yet neither of them could make dinner? Trevor chuckled.

As he made his way to the bathroom, his bones ached a little, probably from trying to sleep in his truck. He had a toothbrush there that he used, before jumping into the shower. His clothes were a mess so he grabbed a pair of sweats from Simon's drawers before walking into the main part of the house to see him sitting at the table.

"I got dinner," he said sadly.

"Thanks." Food could wait, though. Something weighed heavily on Simon's mind. Trevor could practically see the anchor there, pulling him down.

"Your eye and the side of your face is black and blue."

Trevor shrugged, still standing a few feet away from Simon. "I've been worse."

There was a short pause before Simon spoke. "My dad never really cared whether I was around or not. It wasn't that he was abusive. I always had food to eat, and a roof over my head, but…I don't think he ever wanted to be a father. He definitely didn't sign on to be a single father. I always knew that—that she'd wanted me, so he'd given me to her, and then my mom died, leaving him to take care of the kid he didn't know how to love."

Trevor walked over to Simon, pulled one of the kitchen chairs in front of him, and sat. He didn't speak, didn't ask Simon to continue or what happened next. He let the man go at his own pace. He had all the time in the world to wait.

"He never picked out birthday or Christmas gifts because he didn't know me well enough to know what I would want. I always got money or gift cards. He worked all day, and I went to school. We'd eat frozen dinners every night while he watched TV and had one beer. It was never more than that, just the one beer, and TV before he'd go to bed, and then we'd start over again.

"He didn't go to parent-teacher nights. 'You don't need that, right Simon? I know you're doing fine,' was his excuse. I always told him it was okay, but I wanted him to go. I just wanted to know he cared that I was there. I did well in school because it was something I had that he didn't. He'd dropped out of high school and told me he'd wished he'd gone to college. I always thought if I did well in school, and went on to do something with my life, then maybe I would matter to him."

Trevor closed his eyes and shook his head. No matter how much he'd screwed up in his life, he always knew he mattered to his mom and Blake. Even with things strained between himself and his brother, he knew they cared.

"I didn't get the chance. He died my senior year of high school—heart attack. He'd worked himself into the ground his whole life. He never got to see me make something of myself."

But Simon had never stopped trying to be a person his father could love, had he? And he'd tried to honor him in death by fixing broken hearts. Jesus, Trevor respected the man.

"I care." Trevor shrugged. "You matter to me." And he did. More than Trevor ever thought he would...he was falling in love with Simon. Hell, maybe he was already there.

***

Trevor's words should make him want to run. This was never in his plan, caring about someone again. He hadn't done well with it the first time...and he wasn't doing so hot this time, either. But he didn't feel the need to escape. Not from this.

"I know you do. That's why I hate that I left last night. I should have been there for you, should have supported you. I was shit at that with Heather too."

"Don't," Trevor cut him off. "Don't compare me to your ex-wife. Her and I aren't the same. I don't think you're the same as you used to be, either."

That wasn't true, though. If he wasn't the same, Simon wouldn't have run off while Trevor was in the bathroom.

"I don't know how to do this."

"And I do? I'm still trying to figure out how to keep myself from drowning in a bottle most days."

He loved that honesty in Trevor. It was something Simon wasn't sure he ever had. "There's a surgery. It's new and controversial…but it could help me, yet I'm too scared to do it. If it doesn't work then I know there really is no chance. You're still living, you're fighting your demons every day. I'm running from my fears." That hurt to admit. Simon had always considered himself a strong man…but he didn't feel that anymore. There was something to be said for someone showing you your weaknesses. Not in a way that belittled him, but in a way that made Simon see more clearly. That's what Trevor gave him.

"You'll do it when you're ready. You knew I was sober this morning before you saw me, and I know this about you. I guess this just proves you're human like the rest of us. I looked you up, you know. All that shit you've done…they say you were a young genius."

Simon laughed, feeling lighter but wanting more. Wanting Trevor. He'd never been enough for his father. Heather loved him, he knew that, but he also knew there were parts of him that checked the boxes of what she'd wanted from a husband. Someone like her father. And then…well, then he hadn't been able to give her what she needed. No baby. He hadn't been able to be there for her the way she needed, either.

"I want you." Probably more than he ever had. Simon didn't look away from Trevor. "I know you're sore and—"

"Shut up. It was a fight. I'm not dying. I'd be insulted if you didn't want me right now. I kicked ass last night. Isn't that a turn on?"

Simon laughed like only Trevor could make him. Then he stood, and said, "Let's go."

CHAPTER TWENTY-NINE

Trevor didn't feel any pain, not anymore. He felt desire, need, and hunger. As soon as they got to Simon's room he pulled the man's shirt off, kissing his neck, Adam's apple, collarbone, and chest. He loved a firm, masculine body. Loved the feel of rough hair against his face, and muscle under skin.

He'd never lacked for sex. Never. Not since he lost his virginity as a teenager. But it was always just that…sex. Drunk sex, high sex, fast sex. This was different. Trevor wanted to savor it. Wanted to let Simon fuck him all day, every day just because it felt real. Drugs were good at numbing you…making it so nothing felt real. Everything was real with Simon.

His hands moved down to unsnap Simon's pants, only to realize he was already doing it himself. He had them unbuttoned and unzipped before Trevor had the chance. Simon shoved his own jeans down, stepping out of them while he pushed his hands down the back of Trevor's sweats.

His finger slid down Trevor's crack, making him shiver. It was nothing compared to the overwhelming need he felt when Simon whispered against his ear, "I want to use my tongue on you…want to taste you the way you do me. I want to fuck you with my tongue."

Simon definitely enjoyed Trevor rimming him, and he loved driving Simon crazy that way, loved his face between Simon's cheeks while he went wild, but this? Hell yes, he wanted to feel Simon do the same thing to him. "About time," he teased before cupping Simon's balls, wrapping a hand around his rod, and stroking once before climbing onto the bed.

He went down on his stomach, hips slightly off the bed, ass in the air and legs spread. Simon lay on him, their bodies aligned, a hand in Trevor's still shower-wet hair.

"I don't understand it…what you do to me…" He thrust, his cock sliding up and down Trevor's ass crack, while he kissed Trevor's neck. "I think about you all the time. I want you all the time. I don't want to fail you."

"You won't. We'll figure it out." Trevor pushed backward, trying to get his ass as close to Simon as he could. Yeah, he wanted the tongue Simon promised him, but right now, he just needed to be close in whatever way he could. Simon could fuck him right now, no foreplay, and he'd be okay with it.

"Fuck me or eat me, Simon. If you don't, I'm doing it to you."

Simon chuckled into his neck before pushing off of Trevor. He lay between Trevor's legs, one hand rubbing Trevor's ass cheek, a finger tracing his taint. "Your ass is so sexy. Your hole…so fucking sexy." It wasn't said with confidence the way Trevor would say it to Simon. It was with surprise…almost unsure, not in the desire but in a way that made Simon sound unsure of himself.

"Show me how much you want it," Trevor told him. If not he'd end up jerking himself off. He needed something and he needed it now.

"Impatient."

"Passionate."

Simon laughed. "That too."

Trevor couldn't help but twitch when Simon's tongue ran the length of his crack. He spread his legs more, opened himself up for Simon as best he could.

He already felt so damn hard that he could come, but when Simon's face was there, his tongue running back and forth over his sensitive rim, it got kicked up to a whole other level.

His tongue moved quickly as it flicked over Trevor. He pushed back, rode the bed, and gave Simon his ass at the same time. "Finger me, then give me your tongue."

He was already wet with Simon's saliva but he still heard Simon suck on his finger before working it into Trevor's hole. He liked that, the feeling of someone inside him, fucking him and taking him.

Trevor reached back with his hands, face in the pillows as he spread his ass wider for Simon. He wanted to feel him as close as he could.

Simon pulled back slightly. "I love having you like this. Seeing you laid out for me, strong…all that rock solid muscle as you go crazy for me."

He shoved his tongue between Trevor's cheeks at that, using it along with his finger to fuck Trevor.

Trevor moved his hips, fucking the bed, needing friction. "You're gonna make me come, baby. If you want me to come while you're inside of me, you need to stop." He could hardly get the words out. Part of him hoped that Simon wouldn't stop. He could fuck Trevor afterward. He had no doubt he could get hard again and come with Simon inside of him as well.

But then Simon pulled back. His movements were rushed, almost frantic with need as he grabbed lube and condoms from the drawer. Trevor lay where he was, waiting, watching Simon get ready to take him…but then he smiled down at Trevor, before lying beside him.

"I want you to have me. Fuck me, Trevor."

***

Trevor looked at him with shocked eyes. Simon could tell he hadn't expected those words. Simon hadn't really expected to say them. He wasn't sure why. It wasn't something that he was afraid of. It wasn't even something they'd talked a lot about. Trevor just automatically bottomed for him. It was reflex. Probably because he knew Simon had never bottomed. But he didn't fear it. He wanted it. With Trevor.

"It should have been the other way around then, my tongue in your ass." Trevor traced a finger up and down Simon's erection. His eyes rolled back in his head, the simple touch felt so good.

"I wanted to taste you too. Want both."

"Greedy, aren't you?" Trevor then used his finger on Simon's crown.

"Complaining?" He really needed Trevor to hurry before he embarrassed himself.

“Hell no.” Trevor rolled on top of him, their cocks touching as he took Simon’s mouth. He didn’t go slow or easy, pushing his tongue inside, dominating the kiss.

And Simon let him.

He wrapped his arms around Trevor, palming his ass as they moved in unison, fucking each other’s mouths.

It was so different, the feel of Trevor’s body against him. The other men he’d been with, they hadn’t been built like Trevor—hard muscle.

They both moved together, kissing and rubbing their dicks against each other. It was a stupid game to play. Pre-come leaked from his head, but he couldn’t stop, either.

Until Trevor made the decision for him.

He pulled Simon down the bed slightly, taking his head off the pillows before shoving one under his hips. He kneeled between Simon’s legs, then took the lube and coated his finger. Trevor leaned forward again, another hard kiss before his cold, wet finger circled Simon’s hole.

His first instinct was to tense up, but he caught himself before Trevor could tell him to relax…he moved…trying to get his ass closer to Trevor. They’d danced around this long enough.

Trevor took the hint, pushing a finger inside, tongue in Simon’s mouth as his finger took his hole.

And then there was another one there, stretching him, moving inside him. They didn’t stop kissing the whole time.

He kept going, stretching Simon, getting him ready, until, “We can go slow next time. I’m going to lose my mind if I don’t get inside you soon."

"Then do it. I'm waiting." Simon tried to sound as though he wasn't nervous. He wanted this. He wasn't scared, but it was new.

Trevor ripped open the condom wrapper and rolled it on. He was big, thick. It would be a big adjustment over the two fingers he'd just had.

Trevor kneeled on his legs, knees bent in front of him. He lubed himself and Simon before pulling Simon closer. Simon was still on his back, but when Trevor pushed Simon's legs up, close to his chest.

"I'm good at this, I promise." He winked at Simon and then leaned forward, eased Simon's legs back more, and pushed inside. It burned, stretched. He felt full, too full, and then… "You got it, baby. I'm almost in. I'll fuck you good." He leaned forward more, making it easier to get inside Simon.

Pleasure rolled through him, loosened him up, and that's when Trevor started to fuck. The burn edged to nothing but pleasure. "Christ, that feels incredible." Out of his mind good.

"Hold your legs," Trevor told him and Simon did. It was then that Trevor wrapped a hand around Simon's erection; he was wet with lube as he jacked Simon off—jacked him off and fucked him.

Their bodies were slick with sweat as Trevor leaned over him, hammering into Simon over and over. Each thrust went straight to his balls, making them want to explode. He wanted to let loose. To let go.

Trevor adjusted his thrusts, changed the angle just as his hand squeezed tighter on Simon's prick. One squeeze, and a rope of come shot from him. Trevor pumped again, and another jetted out, then another, before Trevor tensed above him. He let go, his face a look of pleasure and concentration as he came in two long thrusts inside of Simon.

"We'll figure it out," Trevor said again as he lay on top of Simon. Simon kissed the bruise on the side of his forehead.

They would. Whatever was going on—their relationship, where it went from here, getting over their issues, they'd find a way to figure it out.

CHAPTER THIRTY

Neither Trevor nor Blake ever mentioned their fight. That's how it went with them. Every time Trevor let Blake down, they acted like it never happened. He had no idea who was letting who down this time, but they fell into the easy rut of pretending things were fine.

They worked together and laughed together. It wasn't like they steered clear of each other. They had dinner with their mom another night—where Trevor had to make up an excuse for his bruised face—but no matter how much they acted like nothing had happened, it was always there. Trevor felt it, and he had no doubt that Blake did as well.

The weeks turned into another month, and then six weeks. It was near the end of August, and they were about a week away from finishing Simon's house. Trevor had never been so nervous in his life. This was Simon's home, his *home,* that he'd trusted Trevor with, and he didn't want to fuck that up.

"That paint shade doesn't look right. Are you sure the painter is using the right one? I don't think that's what Simon ordered." He ran a hand through his hair and looked at his brother, who smiled while shaking his head at Trevor.

Jason walked up and put an arm around Blake. "We're not going to fuck up your boyfriend's house, Trev. Breathe."

"Fuck you. I'm breathing. It has nothing to do with it being Simon." They all knew that was a lie.

He'd been on edge like that the past couple weeks. The closer they got to finishing, the more he worried it wasn't right…the more he wondered where they would go from there. In reality, he knew his relationship with Simon had nothing to do with him remodeling Simon's home, but Trevor had also never had someone in his life that he gave a shit about like Simon. It made him start worrying about everything.

He tried to hide it. Of course, Simon noticed him being on edge. For the past six weeks, Trevor had spent almost every night at Simon's place. The man would have to be dense not to notice, and if there was one thing he knew about Simon, it was that he was a smart man.

Plus, he hadn't let Simon into the house in a week. It surprised him that Simon listened, but as far as Trevor knew, he hadn't stepped foot inside. It wasn't the way things were supposed to go. It could get them in a whole hell of a lot of trouble if there was a problem. Blake didn't get it, but that's the way Trevor wanted it and Simon seemed okay with it.

He didn't tell Simon the day they finished the house. The next morning they got up, went on their run, and then Trevor showered and got ready for work like he always did. When it was time to walk up the hill to the other house, he nodded at the door. "Get your ass up there."

Simon smiled. "Oh, I'm allowed in my own home again?"

"You are." Trevor opened the door and they walked together up the hill. The outside wasn't done. The painters still had to come and finish that up, and the yard needed a serious overhaul, but the inside, Trevor's part, was done.

"Anything can be fixed if it looks different than you imagined it would. I should have had you come in an approve things close to the end but—"

"You're worried." Simon's brows pulled together.

"I'm a recovering drug and alcohol addict who didn't go to college, and who just remodeled his doctor-boyfriend's house. This, building you this home, it's all I have to give to you. Of course, I'm nervous." He didn't like it but it was the truth. Trevor wasn't a prize. He came with more baggage than most people. In a lot of ways, he would always be a gamble, because recovery was a lifetime thing. Simon not only risked more by being with Trevor than Trevor did by being with him, but he also gave more.

Simon grabbed his hand as they made it to the wraparound porch. "You have a whole hell of a lot more to give than that. Probably more than you know. Show me my house, Trev."

Trevor led him inside and did just that.

***

Simon couldn't stop taking it all in—from the built-in bookshelves to the hardwood floors. The open space that, before, had been blocked off by too many walls. It was exactly the place he'd needed when he wanted the house remodeled—a place he would be content, and not have to leave if he didn't want to.

He wasn't sure he'd realized that at first but he did now. He'd made it everything he wanted, because this was what he could control.

Trevor showed him his office and library last. He pushed opened the double doors he'd chosen, dark mahogany with designs engrained along the edges, and… Wow. "It's beautiful, Trevor." The shelves went floor to ceiling, unlike the ones downstairs. The fireplace was completely gutted and redone to match the dark theme Simon had chosen for the room.

There was one thing in here that wasn't his, though. None of his belongings or furniture were in the house, but… "How do you know I don't have one?" He touched the oversized desk. It matched the door, old-world, gorgeous edges, and completely Simon.

"I guess I didn't. If you do, now you have two."

Simon looked back and smiled at him. "Even if I had one before, I wouldn't have two. Only this one." Because it was Simon, more Simon than anyone else would have known.

And Trevor had given it to him.

"It's the perfect place to write your book." Trevor stared at him, those blue eyes of his steely on Simon. It had been a discussion often between them. Trevor asked when he was going to start it, and Simon always had an excuse.

"It is." He sat on it, and Trevor walked over and stood between his legs.

"I'm a slave driver. You have no excuses now." He paused and said, "Unless you go back to work."

Simon closed his eyes. He didn't want to go there right now. He just wanted to focus on Trevor.

"I have a question for you."

He knew Trevor would ask regardless of what he said, so Simon looked at him and waited.

"Why not go back to work? You're a doctor, regardless if you're a heart surgeon or not."

He wasn't the first to say that, and logically Simon knew it was true, but… "I'm a surgeon. It's what I want to do." But that wasn't the whole truth, was it? Simon had always been good at that, hiding from the truth and his emotions. Trevor made it nearly impossible. "I don't know if I can do it…be the doctor I was, if I lost my favorite part of it. I'm afraid I don't have it in me. It feels like failing. Like a consolation prize."

That was about as much as he wanted to get into that. Somehow Trevor knew it because he said, "Want me to give you a blowjob on your new desk? Blowjobs always help."

Simon laughed. "They do, but I have something to ask you, now." His pulse sped up and he suddenly felt hot. Trevor put one hand on each of Simon's legs and waited.

Simon almost said these words fifty times in the past couple weeks. Each time, he'd chickened out. He almost closed them off now, too, but damn, he wanted this. Holding it back wasn't an option anymore. "Move in with me. Here. In this house."

He felt Trevor tense up. "It's a big step."

It was, and he couldn't believe he wanted to do it—share his space, his everyday life with someone, but then this wasn't just someone. It was

Trevor. He'd lost so many other things in his life, and he wanted to hold onto this. "We practically live together anyway."

Trevor's brows pulled together. When he spoke next, Simon wasn't prepared for what he said. "I'm in love with you. You should know that. I've never been in love before, but I'm in love with you."

He opened his mouth, expecting the same words to come tumbling out. He wasn't good at them, though. Trevor was only the second person in his life he'd heard them from. Definitely not his father. The only person he'd said it to in his life was Heather. And even with her he didn't say it as much as a good husband should.

But he thought he felt them…didn't he? He felt the love. Hell, he wanted Trevor to move in with him. He wanted Trevor with him every night. He wanted to make Trevor proud. Trevor supported him in ways Simon couldn't thank him for. He… All those thoughts were there, filling him up but Simon couldn't voice them. Not really. "I'm going to need your help. I've decided to have the surgery on my hand. I can't do it without you. Move in with me, Trev. You said you used to want this house when you were a kid, that you wanted to get a dirt bike and ride it out back; you can do that now. You missed out on too much. Take what you want now. I want to help give it to you."

It was a coward's way out, putting it off the way he did, but Simon still had to work through everything he felt, too. It was the best he could do right now. How could Trevor not see how much more he gave than Simon did?

Trevor waited, watched him as though he thought he could see inside Simon. Hell, maybe he could. "You get the surgery on your hand. I'll stay here and take care of you. If that goes well, I'll move in."

He let the air out of his filled lungs. It had been all he could give, but somehow it turned out to be enough.

CHAPTER THIRTY-ONE

Simon had a few appointments in San Francisco over the next couple weeks. Trevor didn't go with him to those, but he did stay at Simon's house while he was gone. There was no reason for him not to go ahead and move in with Simon. He practically lived there already, only going home to get clothes every few days.

Something held him back, though. Maybe it was that Blake wouldn't understand, and he was tired of fighting with his brother. They did well at work every day (they'd taken a new job), but the tension was still always there.

Blake aside, it was a big step, and big steps scared him. What if he wasn't ready? What if he relapsed? What if Simon had to deal with living with an addict the way his mom and Blake had? The thought of putting Simon through that made him sick. The thought of becoming the person he used to be scared him to death.

So he still pretended like Simon having the surgery would give him some clarity. Like it would change something inside of Trevor, when it couldn't.

He knew what he wanted—Simon. He just had to make sure his head was on straight.

When the doctors in the city decided Simon was a good candidate for the procedure, he knew he had to say something to his family…because he would be leaving with Simon for a few days. Because he would need time off. Because he was in love with Simon, and maybe he owed it to his family to show them how serious Trevor was about him.

It was the first time he'd ever really been serious about anything other than his sobriety and Rock Solid. The construction company was so much a part of his brother as well, Trevor wasn't sure if that counted.

He waited until after they'd finished eating dinner at his mom's house to say, "I need to talk to you guys for a minute."

Trevor tried to ignore the concerned looks in both their eyes as they all took a seat in the living room—Trevor and his mom on the beige couch, with Blake on the chair across from them.

He rubbed his hands together, trying not to be nervous but he couldn't help that he was. What if he wasn't ready? This could go really fucking wrong.

"I'm in love with Simon," Trevor blurted out. There was probably an easier way for him to lead into it but there it was.

Blake didn't move, just continued sitting there, elbows on knees, watching him. It was their mom who spoke. "Does he feel the same?" She sounded worried as hell. He got that. It wasn't like Trevor had ever done anything the easy way, and Simon hadn't made the best impression.

"Don't know." Trevor shrugged. He'd told Simon and Simon hadn't said it back. “He asked me to move in with him.”

“You live there already,” Blake cut in.

“You know what I mean.”

“Oh, Trevor.” His mom leaned closer, and hugged him. “I’m happy for you. That’s the news any mom wants to hear.”

She didn’t have to say the “but” for Trevor to hear it.

“Are you sure you aren’t moving too quickly? It’s only been a few months. You have Rock Solid, and your sobriety needs to be the most important aspect of your life right now. Have you really thought this through?”

He got why she would ask. When had he ever really thought anything through? But this, he did. Maybe after everything he’d done, Trevor didn’t really deserve this piece of happiness, but he wanted it. “Yeah, yeah I’m sure. I’m doing everything I can to make the right decisions. I’m doing everything in my power to be a good man. I haven’t missed a meeting, and I haven’t slipped up—not once. I go to work. I do all the shit I didn’t do before. Don’t I deserve to be happy too?”

Her eyes pooled with tears and she smiled. Trevor let out a deep breath. He needed this. Needed their support because he was scared to death of fucking this up.

“Of course you do. You’re right.” She hugged him again, and they continued talking. Trevor told them he hadn’t said yes yet but he would. They spoke about the surgery, and since the job they were working on was small, it was okay for him to take a few days off. Blake replied when he should, and agreed when he needed to, but he was pissed. Trevor could always read his brother. Still, he waited until they got home to confront him.

Trevor held his arms out and then let them fall again. "Let me have it. I know you want to. Tell me everything I'm doing wrong, and how you would do it better. Oh, and don't forget all the ways I'll screw up in the future." He was so tired of this shit. So fucking tired of fighting and defending himself.

Blake shrugged. "I got nothing, man. You just do whatever you gotta do, and I'll be here waiting to help you put your shit back together when it falls apart."

Anger took control of Trevor's muscles, made his feet move, so he took a step forward and his arms lifted to push his brother. Blake stumbled backward but caught his footing easily. "Fuck. You. I never asked you for shit. You're the one who came to me about Rock Solid. You're the one who said we should get a place together. I'm not stupid. I know it's because you think you need to babysit me, but don't put that shit on me! I never asked you to do it."

Blake got right in his face, hot breath against Trevor's skin. "Did you ever think it's because I missed my brother?" He pushed Trevor back, but Trevor didn't advance on him again. He stood there, breathing heavily, his chest aching from the pain in Blake's eyes. They reminded him of the hurt he'd seen in his own too many times. Of the hurt he'd put in his brother's or his mother's eyes more than he ever wanted to do. "You were my best friend. No matter what, I always had my big brother. We did everything together, and then I lost you because you chose drugs over family. You're my *twin.* Maybe you were too fucked up to feel that loss, but I wasn't, Trev. I fucking felt it."

Blake shook his head, locked his hands together behind his neck, elbows out, and looked down. "It was different in the beginning. When you first got out of rehab, I couldn't let myself believe you would stick with it because I didn't want to be let down again. Just when I started to believe it, just when I got my brother back, you traded one addiction for another—drugs for Simon. You do that, man, make your life all about one thing." he shrugged. "I guess I was just hoping for a little time with my brother. Not the guy we had for all those years you were using, but the real Trevor. I get it, though. You deserve to be happy. Move on with your life. Whatever you need. I'll just keep living in your shadow."

Blake turned and headed for the hallway, and his bedroom. For a minute, Trevor stood there, unable to breathe. Was it true? Did he really put all his energy into one thing? Did he move from drugs to Simon? He didn't think so…but then, what had he done with Blake outside of work? Or Jason. They'd invited him. There were things they could do that didn't involve partying. He believed it was because he couldn't handle how they looked at him, but was he fooling himself? Using it as an excuse?

"I asked you to go jogging with me. I wanted you to." Jogging? That's all he could come up with?

Blake didn't respond.

But then, Trevor let Blake's words sink in, really sink in, and heard them. "You really feel that way? Like you live in my shadow?" How in the hell could Blake feel that way? He was the good one. He was the one who never screwed up. He was the one Trevor should model his behavior after.

Blake stopped walking and stood in front of his door. "I was never like you. I was more cautious, which meant not as much fun. People flocked to you, they loved you. The only person who wanted me over you was Jace. And that's just because…" He crossed his arms and turned to face Trevor. "You're only six minutes older than me, but you always felt like my big brother. I always wanted to be like you. I only had the balls to admit I was gay after you did. I was always the boring one, and you were the fun one. That was okay because we were a team. We had each other. It hurt to lose that, man. I just wanted my brother back."

Damned if Trevor's eyes didn't go blurry. Somehow he'd missed it all. "I felt the same way about you. Christ, Blake, I couldn't do anything without knowing I had you with me. It was easy for me to come out because I knew you were, too. You think I could have done that shit alone? I always wanted to be like you—smart, determined, responsible. I was the fuck-up who couldn't do shit without his little brother. I still can't."

They stood twenty-five feet away from each other, their eyes never diverting.

"It's hard to be around you because I don't want to let you down anymore. There's nothing I hate more than letting you down," Trevor admitted.

"You don't have to be perfect. I just want my brother."

Trevor moved toward his brother, and pulled him into a hug. He couldn't even remember the last time he hugged him. "You have me, man. We're a team. Always."

They still had things to figure out. Trevor needed to put some serious thought into Blake's words…if he was right about Trevor putting all of his energy into one thing. But they were okay. For the first time in a long time, Trevor and his brother were okay.

CHAPTER THIRTY-TWO

"This is where you used to work?" Trevor looked at the sign for Roosevelt Heart and Vascular Institute in San Francisco.

"I was the head surgeon here, yes."

"Oh, not just *a* surgeon here, the *head* surgeon." Trevor tried to laugh it off, but looking at this place, really thinking about the things Simon had done—cutting people open to fix their hearts—he felt like they were in two different worlds. In the beginning, he focused on that more, but as they spent more time together, the differences didn't matter. They weighed heavily on Trevor today, though. They felt bigger than they used to.

"Yes. I was good, Trevor. Extremely good." He leaned back in the driver's seat of his car and looked out the window. "God, I miss it. I miss it so much some days I feel like I can't breathe. How many people in the world get to do what I did? I healed people's hearts. I might not have been in touch with mine, but I sure as hell could do miracles with other people's." There was a longing in Simon's voice that hit Trevor straight in the chest. It wasn't often that Simon opened himself up like that. It wasn't often he sounded so passionate about anything.

"You'll get it back. If not, you'll realize that you can still perform miracles, even if you can't operate. You're a fucking doctor, Simon. That's incredible." Trevor believed that. He'd never done anything that mattered like that.

Simon let his eyes travel away from the building and to Trevor. "Thank you."

Trevor shrugged. "Regardless of that whole doctor thing, you always get to say you're fucking the best looking man in California. There's always that." He winked and Simon laughed. It was a long shot, trying to make Simon laugh, but Trevor was glad it worked.

"Yeah, there's always that." He paused for a second before adding, "I need to go in."

"I know." And Simon might not want Trevor to go with him. He understood that. This was Simon connecting with his past—the place where he performed miracles and dated women.

Simon got out of the car, walked around the vehicle, and made it to the sidewalk before he stopped. Trevor watched him as he kept his back to Trevor…and he waited. Either way, he was okay with what Simon decided.

Still, when Simon turned around and nodded at the building, Trevor felt a rush of adrenaline that he wanted Trevor by his side. The man who had done things Trevor could only dream about wanted him.

***

"Wow. Look who it is. It's great to see you, Simon." Lin Pham, one of his associates, reached out and shook Simon's hand. The one he was hoping to fix.

"I'm in town for a surgery. I thought I would stop by to see how things are going."

Lin smiled at him. "It's great, but we sure miss you. It's not the same without you. We miss your expertise, and the patients are still asking about Dr. Malone. They all love you." Simon got a sharp pain in his chest, an ache that had dulled but never really went away. The longing for what he had. For what he wanted.

"I miss it too," was all he could say. Then he realized he hadn't introduced Trevor so he looked his way. "Trevor, this is Dr. Lin Pham, Lin this is my…" Holy shit. He hadn't thought about that. How did he introduce Trevor. As his lover? Boyfriend? The second one made him feel like he was sixteen years old. Plus, they'd all known about Heather, and now he was introducing a man as his…whatever the word should be.

Trevor jumped in and saved him. "I'm his friend, Trevor. It's nice to meet you, Dr. Pham." He reached out and shook her hand.

"Please, call me Lin. Any friend of Simon's is a friend of mine."

Simon could see the questions there, probably only because of his stumble on how to introduce Trevor. What really bothered him was whether or not he cared if Lin knew. He shouldn't. There was nothing to be ashamed of, but he still couldn't decide how he felt about it.

"Where are you working? I heard you moved. Did you start a practice somewhere else?" she asked. Because that's what most people would do. Continue being a physician, surgeon or not. But not Simon, and for the first time he felt slightly embarrassed about that.

"No, not yet. I'm working on a book right now." He didn't look at Trevor, who knew he was lying. Another dose of embarrassment settled into his bones. He had no excuses not to start his book. None at all.

Before Lin could reply he heard another voice. "Dr. Malone! It's so great to see you!" Linda, one of the medical assistants, approached him. Then another, and a member of the registration staff, all of them telling Simon how much they missed him. How good of a physician he was, and asking what he was doing now.

Somehow, without realizing it, he'd been close with his staff, and he hadn't spoken to any of them since he realized he couldn't go back to work.

It felt good to talk with them now. He missed this, being part of a team. Of a group, all working together to save lives.

They spoke for as long as time allowed, talking and laughing, before they had to get back to their responsibilities. It wasn't until they all went their own ways that he realized Trevor was gone.

"Hey. You okay?" Simon asked when he made it back outside and saw Trevor standing there waiting for him.

"Yeah, I just needed a little air." He had his hands deep in the pockets of his jeans.

"I'm sorry about the introduction. I didn't know what to say." And he hadn't taken the time to introduce Trevor to anyone other than Lin, either. It wasn't done purposely, but intent didn't matter. The result did. And by not introducing Trevor, he sent a message he didn't mean to send.

"No problem. I get it. Where to next?" There was a slight difference in Trevor's voice, a little more monotone than usual.

"Hey." Simon reached out and latched a finger with Trevor, who shook his head.

"I'm fine. It was nothing."

Simon took his word for it. "I need to get to my pre-op, and then Heather's place." He still couldn't believe he'd agreed to stay at his ex-wife's house with his current male lover. It felt like a mess waiting to happen, but Heather had insisted. She wanted to meet Trevor, and he at least owed her that.

"Let's do this." Trevor walked to the car without looking at him. Simon paused for a second, unsure if he needed to apologize to him again, before he went to the driver's side and got in.

CHAPTER THIRTY-THREE

Half of the people at the hospital knew who Simon was. They got stopped every few minutes as they went to take care of Simon's business.

Sometimes Simon would introduce him—his friend Trevor; other times he would forget. Trevor didn't really take offense to it. He was sure this all had to be overwhelming for Simon—both having Trevor tag along with him, and the fact that he was seeing people he'd worked with for so long. People he'd cut himself off from.

Most of them were nice enough. He got a few sideways looks, confusion over why he was there, and total shock on the look of one man who asked what Trevor did. Apparently construction wasn't as respectable as what Simon did, but that didn't bother him, either. He'd done nothing but use drugs before, and now he had a career, so Trevor was proud of that.

What did make his gut twist was Simon. He was happy, smiling in a way Trevor had never seen from him. Trevor always loved that he could make Simon smile or laugh, but it was nothing compared to how he looked being in this building and talking to these people. He wondered if this was the old Simon. He'd said he was never good with people, but watching him now, Trevor didn't see that. It could be the atmosphere, the excitement, or the fact that he felt closer to being the man he wanted, talking shop between the walls of the hospital. Whatever the reason, half of the time, Trevor sat back in awe of the man he saw, and the other realizing that he didn't fit here.

Simon had told him a million times how much he loved being a surgeon, but hearing it was nothing compared to seeing it. This was who Simon really was. It was who he should be…not the man hiding out in his house, in a small town, with his lover.

It was after five when they made it to Heather's house (which was about three times the size of Simon's in Rockford Falls) and Trevor was really wishing they'd decided to stay in a hotel. He'd much rather spend the evening fucking away the day instead of meeting Simon's ex-wife, and experiencing another part of Simon's life where he didn't really mesh.

Now they sat in the idling car in front of her place.

"Can we make a run for it?" Trevor asked.

"No way. She's probably watching us out the window right now. We'll never make it. Why did we do this?" Simon looked at him.

"Me? *I* didn't do this. That was you, Dr. Malone." Simon smiled at Trevor before he reached out and wrapped a hand around the back of Trevor's head.

"Thank you for being here with me today. I know I don't always handle things the best way. I should have included you more. I should have admitted who you are to me." He pulled and Trevor went easily, returning Simon's kiss. Maybe things weren't as awkward as they felt today. Maybe Trevor had no real reason to feel like he was losing Simon.

***

Simon hadn't even considered that Heather would have Alan over tonight. Sure enough, an hour into being at their house, her fiancé, and Simon's previous colleague, showed up for dinner.

"Thanks for the heads-up," Simon said to her since the two of them were alone in the kitchen.

"Does it matter?"

Simon's eyes darted away when she spoke, and then, "You're keeping him a secret, Simon? Holy shit. You asked the man to move in with you and you're keeping him a secret."

"No. He's not a secret." He wasn't. Was he?

"Then why in the hell would it matter if Alan is here? Oh my God. You introduced Trevor as your friend out there. I didn't realize. What the hell is wrong with you?" She slapped Simon's arm.

"Christ. Nothing. Nothing is wrong with me. How am I supposed to introduce him? As the man I asked to go steady with me?" While he defended himself he knew she was right. "People could tell. I know they were surprised—because he's a man, and because he's younger…" Pierced and tattooed… "When they asked Trevor what he did."

"So? And you realize you're making yourself sound like more of an asshole by the second, don't you? You're hiding your boyfriend not only because he's a man, but you're also an ageist, and apparently stuck up because you're the great Dr. Malone and he's a construction worker."

Fear and guilt ate through his defense. "Don't. That's not it." And then, "Is it?" But he knew it wasn't. Not really. Simon respected the hell out of Trevor. He respected the man more than anyone he knew. What Simon did—school, studying, becoming a surgeon—those were things most people could do if they put their minds to it. What Trevor was doing—staying sober, starting over—that took guts Simon never had.

The truth was, he was scared to death. Not because of who Trevor was or their differences. Those were just easy excuses to use. "I've never felt about anyone the way I feel about him." There was a brief flash of pain in her eyes, and he realized maybe that wasn't the best thing to say to his ex-wife. "I'm sorry."

"It's okay. Go on."

"He's…Christ, he's strong. He's been through more than you realize, and he doesn't give up. He's suffered through more than I have, and we both know I easily gave up. I care about him deeply, and now being here… I just keep thinking, what if this works? What if this is my miracle and I can operate again? If that's the case, I belong here, and then what happens with Trevor?" Simon hadn't realized he had all of those fears until he voiced them.

"Then you'll figure it out." Heather placed a hand on his arm. "That's what you do when you love someone—you figure it out. You don't give up. You make sacrifices for each other." None of which Simon was very good at. None of which he'd done for her. "Just don't block him out, Simon. You're good at leaving the other person alone to try and figure out what's going on by themself. Tell him how you feel, or he's going to think he's doing something wrong. I speak from experience when I say that's not a fun place to be."

No, he couldn't imagine it would be. He hated that he'd put Heather there. He never wanted to do that with Trevor.

Simon grabbed Heather's hand, kissed it, and then gave it a squeeze. "I'm so sorry for everything. I don't know what I would do without you."

She gave him a sad smile. "I guess we're much better at being friends than anything else."

He nodded and gave her another squeeze. "Yeah…yeah, I guess so."

CHAPTER THIRTY-FOUR

Trevor sat next to Simon at the table as they got ready to eat. Alan had gone back out to his car; Trevor wasn't sure why until he came back in.

"I forgot the wine. I have both red and white. Which do you prefer?" Trevor's insides froze. That quickly, just by it being offered, the desire hit. He deserved it, right? After the strangeness of the day. Just a glass of wine with dinner. Most people did that. There shouldn't be anything wrong with that. He should be able to have a fucking glass of wine or a beer with dinner.

"No. We don't want any. Thank you," Simon answered for him, voice tight. "Actually, I'd prefer it if you didn't drink at all."

"It's fine." Trevor grit his teeth. He should be able to do this. He *could* do this. It wasn't as though he'd never been out to a restaurant where people were drinking. Sitting at the table with them while they shared a glass of wine wasn't a big deal.

Simon started, "I—" but then Trevor cut him off.

"It's fine." He really fucking needed this to be fine. He was already so different than Simon in too many ways. He didn't want to be the guy who couldn't go out to dinner with people who were close to Simon because they might have a drink. He didn't want to be the man who held Simon back from that, either.

The room was thick with confusion. This whole trip was full of it, and they still had to get through Simon's surgery.

He noticed that even though Alan and Heather poured themselves small glasses of wine, neither of them drank it. They realized what was going on. It had to be obvious. There was no reason for Simon to have acted the way he did when Alan brought out the wine. They knew he was in recovery. It wasn't something he should feel ashamed about. Most days he was proud as hell about it, but today, he couldn't find it in himself to feel good.

Dinner went well. Alan and Heather were both polite to Trevor. He liked them, felt more comfortable around them than he had anyone else they met today. He could tell they both cared about Simon, which made them care about Trevor. That was an important quality to have.

Still, after dinner, Trevor knew that if he didn't get out of the house for a few minutes he was going to go bat-shit crazy.

He wanted the wine. Wanted something to help take the edge off of their day. He needed something, anything, to help calm him down.

"I'll go with you." Simon started to stand when Trevor said he was going out for some fresh air, but sat again when Trevor shook his head.

"Nah, I'm good. Spend time with your friends. I'll be right back." He squeezed Simon's shoulder, trying to play it off that he felt calmer than he really did.

As Trevor slipped out, Simon got back into his conversation with Alan about medical procedures, or something to that effect.

He realized the bubble had burst. It was easy at home. They spent all their time at Simon's house, running, fucking, and hanging out together. They rarely dealt with people other than Trevor's family, but that was different. This was life, and it made their differences shine so bright, Trevor couldn't ignore them.

Trevor had a lot of shit to deal with.

Simon was a surgeon. He needed to be a surgeon. It's who he was.

He heard a noise behind him, and slowed his steps. He hadn't expected Simon to come out with him. That wasn't typically how his lover operated.

"Hey."

Trevor turned at the female voice behind him. Simon hadn't come. It was Heather.

"Hi," he replied as they fell into step together.

"He's not good at this kind of thing. It doesn't mean he doesn't care. He just wouldn't come out here unless you told him to."

Trevor chuckled. "That's okay. That's the one thing he doesn't have to worry about with me. No mixed signals. If I really wanted him to come out, I would have told him to. I'm a big boy."

He hadn't meant to embarrass her, but the tint to her cheeks told him he had. Trevor only saw it because her driveway was lit up like a damn stadium.

"That makes sense. I would have been pissed if he didn't come out here." The two of them laughed and kept walking. He could tell she was a strong woman, but it became even more apparent when she asked, "How long have you been sober?" It was a bold question, but the sound of her voice was filled with compassion.

"Around a year and a half. Thanks for not beating around the bush."

"I learn quickly." She nudged his arm. He liked her. A lot. "I'm sorry about that. I didn't know. I respect you for what you're doing. It can't be easy."

No, no it wasn't. They stressed that in rehab and at their meetings. That there would always be hard days. That it would always be a struggle, but he didn't realize how true it was until he lived it. "Thank you."

There was more silence between them. She had something on her mind. Trevor wasn't sure if he wanted to hear it or not.

"Can I speak bluntly?" she finally asked.

"Go for it. You have so far." He pushed his hands into his pockets.

"I just…I know this is probably strange, but please, don't give up on him. It's hard for Simon to really connect with other people. Maybe it's because of his dad or being a doctor and keeping that wall up so it doesn't hurt as bad when you lose a patient. I don't know, but it's difficult for him. One thing I know is that he cares about you. The fact that he told me about you proves it. The fact that you're here right now. This surgery? There's no reason he couldn't do it alone. He'll spend a day in the hospital, if that. He could have stayed here until he could drive or I would have driven him home. He didn't need you…but he *wanted* you. He wouldn't have wanted me here that way." Heather grabbed his hand, squeezed it, then turned and walked back toward the house.

Trevor needed to hear that. He also needed it to be true.

***

They didn't talk much when Trevor got back up to the house. He asked Heather about a shower and she showed him to his and Simon's room.

It was only a few minutes after Trevor went upstairs that Simon said his goodnights.

"We're together," he told Alan, though he knew the man realized that. Still, it felt important to Simon to say it. He hadn't said it all day, when he should have. "I should have introduced him as my partner when you got here." Maybe Trevor didn't care about that. It was a label, a name. They knew who they were to each other, and that's what mattered, but Simon also wanted to be sure no one knew he was ashamed of Trevor. He wasn't.

"He seems like a good man, Simon. And you look happy. Good for you." Alan shook his hand, and Simon thanked him before heading for the stairs.

He pulled out of his shirt when he got to their room, and sat on the foot of the bed, facing the bathroom. He could hear the water running. Thought about going in to join Trevor, but instead he waited.

It didn't take long before the water shut off, and another minute later Trevor stepped out of the bathroom with a towel wrapped around his waist, his hair wet and a mess. Simon wanted to grab onto it. Wanted to lick every one of the ridges of muscle in Trevor's stomach. He wanted to suck the piercing in Trevor's nipple. Wanted to bury his face in the hair at his crotch. Christ, the man was sexy.

"Come here." He used his index finger to wave Trevor over. He came easily, standing between Simon's legs. "I'm not good at this," he admitted.

"We're both going to screw up."

"No. Not with this. I'm the only one screwing up with us. But I'm trying." He trailed a finger down Trevor's chest, and to the edge of his towel before pulling it free. Trevor was hard underneath, a bead of pre-come already at the tip, waiting for Simon. "I'll keep trying, if you let me. Don't…don't give up on me." He'd never said those words to anyone. Not even to Heather about their marriage. But he needed to say them to Trevor.

And then he leaned forward, let his tongue circle the head of Trevor's erection, tasting the salty come there.

He fucking loved it.

Trevor wrapped a hand around the back of Simon's head as Simon took him deep. He sucked hard, tried to swallow around him, the way Trevor did to Simon. He went down as far as he could go, almost gagged, before doing it again. It didn't matter. He just wanted all of Trevor.

Simon held onto Trevor's ass as Trevor thrust gently, making love to Simon's mouth. He smelled the soap on Trevor's skin. The spice and man there, too.

It wasn't long before Trevor's ass cheeks clenched. Before the hand in Simon's hair tightened, and Trevor shot down Simon's throat. He swallowed it all. Would take more. He wanted every part of this man.

Trevor didn't hesitate to lean down and take Simon's mouth. He loved that too. That the man didn't care if he tasted himself on Simon's tongue.

A few minutes later they lay under the covers, naked, with the lights out. Trevor's hand lay on Simon's flaccid cock, just resting it there. This was where Simon should say something. Tell Trevor how much he meant to him, or how much he just might need Trevor, but he didn't have those words. Or he couldn't let them free. Certain parts of him were still locked up too tightly, even though he wanted to free them. "All my paperwork has Heather as my emergency contact and next of kin. I didn't have anyone else, so I kept it. I'd like to change it to you, if you don't mind."

Trevor chuckled quietly, as though it was a stupid question, and maybe it was. "Yeah…yeah, of course. I'd be honored, Simon."

Simon kissed Trevor's forehead before drifting off to sleep.

CHAPTER THIRTY-FIVE

"Trevor…wake up."

Trevor groaned when he felt Simon's warm breath across his cheek, his rough jaw, against his neck. It was the day of Simon's surgery. He knew he needed to get out of bed, but… "This feels too good. Let's stay here all day." Maybe they could hide in this bed the way they hid so often at Simon's house. Things were easier here. Of course Heather might have a problem with it, but he figured they could work around that.

"What will you do to me if I agree to stay here?" Simon asked with mischief that wasn't often in his voice.

"Whatever you want." Trevor rolled over so he faced Simon, but kept his eyes closed. He didn't know why he felt so exhausted.

Trevor went off feel, leaning forward, burying his face in Simon's throat and licking the skin there. "You like my mouth on your ass. I can spend the day with nothing but the taste of you on my tongue—cock, ass, and then cock again. All day. I'll eat nothing but you."

His own prick hardened painfully. That sounded like the perfect day to him, but then, this was important to Simon. It was his life. Trevor needed to be supportive of that. "But we can always do that after your surgery. I'll owe you." Trevor opened his eyes. "I see why you wanted me here now. You don't need my help, you want me to spoil you with sexual favors while you heal."

Trevor laughed and then shifted to get out of bed but Simon pulled him back, bringing Trevor down on top of him.

"What if I don't want to wait?" Simon asked Trevor, a glint in his eyes. He wrapped a hand in Trevor's hair and tugged, pulling Trevor's mouth to his.

Simon's tongue pushed into his mouth, rough and eager. He definitely wasn't complaining. He returned each hard press of lips, each hungry probe of tongues.

"You're going to kill me, Dr. Malone," Trevor said when Simon pulled back. He wanted Simon all the time. Sober sex was the best sex he'd had. *Simon* was the best he'd had.

"Not until I'm done with you. My surgery got postponed a day. What do you say we get out of here? I'd rather you ravage me somewhere other than my ex-wife's house." He gave Trevor a small smile. "We can spend the day together, have a little fun in the city, and then I'm taking you to a beach house I rented for the night. You can eat my ass all night there, as promised."

Jesus, that got to him, hearing Simon talk to him that way. He was so different than Trevor in a lot of ways. He wasn't much of a dirty talker. That was something they needed to work on.

Trevor ground his crotch against Simon's erection. There was no way he wouldn't spend the day doing exactly what Simon said, but he also wasn't above having a little fun with Simon, either. "Only if you tell me exactly what you want me to do to you."

He could practically see Simon stumble over his thoughts. He hadn't expected Trevor to say that. Good.

"I'm listening, doc." He kissed Simon's Adam's apple.

"That tongue of yours…I want to feel it. You said you'd start on my dick, but I want…I want it at my hole. Want your face between my cheeks." Simon tilted his head backward, giving Trevor better access to his throat.

"What else?"

"I want you to lick me until I can't stand it. Use your fingers on me too. I love that, your fingers and tongue inside me."

"Mmm…" He was so close to getting off just listening to Simon talk to him as he kissed Simon and rubbed their bodies together.

"When I'm close to coming," Simon continued. They were both moving now, thrusting against one another. "I'll call you off. You'll roll me over and suck my cock deep, just in time for me to shoot down your throat."

It was then that Trevor's cock jerked. Come pulsed from the slit, pooling between their bodies. Beneath him, Simon shuddered, groaned, and came with Trevor's name on his lips.

As much as he wanted to lie there and never get up again, Trevor shoved out of bed, pulling Simon with him. "What are we waiting for?

Get your ass up. We're going to do everything you just said."

***

Happiness wasn't something Simon really thought about most of his life. He didn't have time for it, not really. He had responsibilities and goals, and to him, those equaled happiness. How could he be happy if he didn't have the things he wanted? What he'd wanted had been his career, more than a person or love so he'd always seen himself as happy.

And maybe he had been in some ways, but as he sat behind the steering wheel, driving to Golden Gate Park, he realized he hadn't had a clue.

Not really.

He was excited. He felt…light. Simon wasn't really sure exactly what the change was. Maybe it had been seeing Heather accept Trevor, or being back in the city. The possibility of what this surgery could give him, seeing his old colleagues, or maybe a combination of all of that.

All he knew was that he'd felt like shit when he'd hurt Trevor at dinner, but he'd felt better after they spoke in the room last night. When the hospital called early this morning about a problem with some equipment and stating that they had to postpone the surgery a day, he should have felt frustrated, but he didn't. Simon felt possibility.

Yesterday hadn't gone how he'd hoped it would, and he wanted to make up for that. He just wanted to try and relax…with Trevor. When did he ever let himself truly relax? Even when he wasn't working, his mind was always going, always on his hand and his career.

It would be back there tomorrow. He had no doubt about that. This was his chance, his shot to get that part of his life back. But today, he had some living to do, too, and he wanted to do it with the man beside him. The man who made him…happy.

"Have you ever been to Golden Gate Park?" Simon asked Trevor when they pulled into the parking garage. There were probably better things he could have taken Trevor to do today, but he also just wanted to hang out. Being here made that possible.

"Nope. I used to only come to San Francisco to buy better drugs, and to hit up better clubs. All I did here was party." He had a tinge of regret in his voice.

Simon reached over and squeezed Trevor's leg. "Not anymore."

"Nope. Not anymore." Trevor rolled his chip around in his hand before shoving it into his pocket. It was security a to him, Simon realized. He'd considered asking to see it numerous times but hadn't, and Trevor never offered.

"What are we going to do first?" Trevor asked as they made their way out of the garage.

Simon knew what he wanted to do, and knew it was slightly ridiculous at the same time.

"You look unsure about something. What are you embarrassed about?" Trevor nudged him.

"You'll have to remember how my mind works." He was stalling. He couldn't believe he was really stalling.

"Spit it out, doc. You're acting like a child."

And announcing where he wanted to go probably wouldn't help with that. "The California Academy of Sciences is here. They have some really interesting exhibits." That wasn't the kind of thing Trevor did. Simon knew that.

"Why are you embarrassed about that? Lead the way."

So Simon did. It took a good couple of hours for them to explore the whole museum. There was a really interesting earthquake exhibit that Simon found fascinating—the how and why of it. All the amazing and scary things the earth could do.

They visited the planetarium next. He hadn't gone to one of these since he was a kid. He remembered his father had dropped him off at one on a Saturday and then picked Simon up a few hours later.

He'd worked all week, he'd told Simon. He was sorry. *You don't need me around, do you?*

Simon had of course told him no when the answer had been yes.

Trevor's favorite part seemed to be the rainforest. It was four levels, and they spent close to an hour exploring every part of it.

It was hot and Simon was sweaty, but the humidity inside didn't seem to bother Trevor.

"Hey, look." Trevor nodded toward the tree in the middle of the circular dome. There was a blue butterfly, one of the brightest Simon had ever seen, resting on a branch right in front of them. "It's beautiful. My mom bought us one of those butterfly kits when we were kids. It came with caterpillars that Blake and I watched until they turned into butterflies. He cried when we had to let them go. I remember busting his balls about it…but I didn't want to let them go, either."

Simon liked hearing these stories from Trevor. It was almost like

Trevor relived them, as if he was finding out new things about himself because he'd been so lost to his addiction for so many years. Simon was lucky as hell that he got to share this with Trevor.

They went to the Conservatory of Flowers and the Japanese Gardens. Trevor rented bikes for them and they rode through the park, exploring every inch of it they could—the lakes, bridges, hills, trees. There was even a part in the park that had American Bison, which they watched for a little while.

It wasn't until they got back to the car that Simon realized something. He'd lived in the city for years, yet he'd never come here, as an adult. Never taken the time. It was such a simple, easy thing to do, yet he'd never done it.

It wasn't only Trevor who was learning new things about himself, Simon was too.

CHAPTER THIRTY-SIX

"Wow. This house is incredible, Simon." Trevor stood in the living room and looked around. It wasn't a large house, not by a long shot. It was close to the size of the guest house on Simon's property, but it had the perfect feel to it. The whole front wall in the living room was windows, facing out to a quiet stretch of beach.

There was no TV. He almost teased Simon about that, but he figured they wouldn't need one anyway. If Trevor had his way, they'd be naked most of the time they were here.

"I'm glad you like it. I was lucky to get it on such short notice." Simon stepped up behind him and massaged Trevor's shoulders. It only lasted a second before Simon pulled back, and Trevor turned to see him rubbing his right hand.

He didn't complain about the pain often, but Trevor knew it bothered him. "I'm supposed to spend the night with my mouth on you, remember?"

Simon smiled. "You won't hear me arguing about that. I'm going to take a quick shower. I feel dirty from our day."

Trevor nodded as Simon went for the hallway. He lasted about two seconds before the blue of the ocean called his name. Trevor found a few towels in the hall closet, grabbed them, kicked out of his shoes and went outside.

It was late evening already. They'd spent their whole day at the park. No one was around, and Trevor couldn't see any houses other than theirs.

This was such an amazing part of living here—the water. Why hadn't he ever let himself experience it before? Probably because he'd been too fucked up.

Trevor pulled off his shirt and kicked out of his shorts, leaving himself in nothing but his boxers. It was cold, and he knew the water would be even colder, but still he went for it.

He made it up to his knees before he started to rethink it. A shiver rocked through him but Trevor kept going. Waves rolled in around him as he dove into the cold water.

He shook his head when he surfaced. It felt good. Cold, but good.

He turned to head back to the shore and saw Simon there, on the sand, with a blanket in his hand. "Come on!" he yelled. "Get your ass out here with me!"

"I'll wait here for you!" Simon called back.

No way. Trevor wasn't accepting that answer. Simon laid the blanket out on the sand as he made his way out of the water.

Simon had his back to Trevor, and he enjoyed the view. His ass beneath his shorts, and the muscles in his back and shoulders moving as he laid the blanket out.

Trevor moved more quickly, and made it to Simon right as he went to turn around, wrapping his arms around Simon from behind. "If you want me to do what I promised, you have to come in the water with me."

Simon shivered. "Going back on your word?"

"Being persuasive." He cupped Simon from behind, hoping like hell to get his wish. Then he unbuttoned Simon's shorts and pulled the zipper down.

"Someone could come out."

"So?" Trevor replied. He pushed Simon's shorts down so he only wore boxer-briefs.

It was getting darker, but not completely night yet. Not too far from where they stood, there was a light for a sidewalk. "This is what we're going to do. You're going to play in the water with me." Trevor cupped him again. "Then we're going to rinse off in the shower by the deck. Then, I'll take you inside and have my way with you, as promised." He let his teeth tease Simon's neck, squeezed his erection, and then backed away.

***

The second Trevor was gone, Simon wanted him back. Trevor gave him no choice except to follow him into the water. And if he was being honest with himself, he'd admit it sounded fun.

He ran after Trevor, who then started running, too, before they both crashed into the waves. He swam after Trevor, grabbed him, and pulled Trevor to him.

Their lips met just as a wave crashed into them, but it didn't stop their kissing.

Christ, this man made him feel alive. Made him feel like a man in a way he'd never felt before. A man with needs and desires and power that was foreign to Simon.

"What is it about you?" Simon asked. He liked having the answers. Where Trevor was concerned, he didn't have them.

"I'm sexy."

And he was, but they both knew it was more than that.

They spent a while holding each other and riding the waves. Simon had felt like he'd freeze his ass off when they first got into the water, but the longer he was here with Trevor, the warmer he got.

"I'm nervous about tomorrow," he admitted after a few minutes of silence.

"It'll be okay. No matter what. I have to believe that. It's what gets me through every day." Trevor grabbed Simon's right hand and kissed the scar there before pulling him out of the water.

They grabbed their things, Simon holding the blanket out away from his body as they went for the showers on the back deck.

He watched as Trevor pulled off his boxers, his tight ass on display under the porch light.

"You're into exhibitionism?" he teased.

"Baby, I'm into everything." Trevor winked at him. Simon stalled a moment before he pulled off his underwear as well. They rinsed the sand off their skin.

The second the water was off, Trevor had his mouth on Simon. It was a frantic, hungry kiss. He shoved his tongue into Simon's mouth and Simon took it. He wanted that hunger. Craved it from Trevor.

"Come on," Simon said when Trevor pulled away, but Trevor only shook his head, smiled, and went down on his knees.

On reflex, Simon's eyes darted around. Anyone could walk by. There were houses not too far down the beach, and a sidewalk between their house and the water.

"I know you like my tongue in your ass. I promised, remember? Turn around and let me keep my promise, doc."

Simon didn't even let himself think about it. He turned, spread his legs, and leaned over the table.

CHAPTER THIRTY-SEVEN

"Jesus, you're sexy. I want you all the time." Trevor ran his hand down the crack of Simon's ass, top to bottom. He fingered Simon's rim before leaning forward and licking between his ass cheeks.

"Want you." Simon pushed back into him, eager for Trevor. He made Trevor feel wanted in a way he had never experienced.

So, he did what he'd promised to do. He rasped his tongue back and forth over Simon's hole. Teased him—hard, soft, then rubbed his finger there.

A dog barked in the distance. Simon froze up, but Trevor didn't. "You move and I stop."

"When did you get so bossy?" Simon asked, but Trevor didn't answer. He only stuck his finger into his mouth, getting it wet before he teased Simon's hole again.

Slowly, he pushed it in, just the first digit, before pulling out again. He went farther the second time.

"Oh, fuck yes," Simon hissed above him, and Trevor couldn't help but smile.

He palmed Simon's ass cheek with one hand, squeezed, and then pushed so Simon got the message. He leaned farther over the table, his chest flat on it, his legs wide to give Trevor better access.

That's when he used his tongue on Simon again, tongue, finger, tongue, finger. He loved this, pleasuring a man. Pleasuring *this* man. He wasn't lying. He could do this all night.

"You asked what it is about me? It's the same for you. Jesus, if you knew what you do to me."

Trevor fucked Simon with both his finger and his tongue. The dog barked again, possibly sounding closer, but Trevor didn't stop licking, didn't stop fingering. Simon's dick didn't touch the table, hanging beneath it and over the edge, making Trevor remember the other part of his promise.

He stroked once, pushed his finger in deeper, looking for Simon's prostate. As soon as he rubbed the spot, Simon jerked, and tensed, moaning.

"I can't believe I never knew about that before you." He rode Trevor's finger, pushing back into him as Trevor touched it again. "Fuck. I'm going to…" Trevor pulled back, pulled his hand away, grabbed Simon's waist and turned him. He covered the head of Simon's prick with his mouth just as the first pulse squeezed out. Another one was right behind it, salty, thick come filling Trevor's mouth.

He sucked the end, wringing it dry before standing.

Trevor leaned forward, kissed the back of Simon's neck and said, "I'm not done with your ass. I want to fuck you. Can I?"

"I'd be disappointed if you didn't."

Simon gave the best fucking answer possible. He went to move, but Trevor told him, "Stay still."

His bag was right inside the doorway to the deck. Trevor went inside, and got a condom and lube.

He ripped open the package with shaky hands. Squeezed lube into his palm, and stroked his condom-covered erection.

"Lean forward again, baby. Yeah. That's it." He lined himself up behind Simon and pushed inside. The second he did, he heard the voices, the dog bark again.

"Shit," Simon whispered, but Trevor just smiled.

"Lean forward a little more." And he did, flat on the table, and Trevor went down over him. In their position he had to stand on his toes to be able to move inside Simon the way he wanted, but he made it work—slow, deep movement, their bodies touching nearly everywhere.

"Christ, that feels good. Right there." Simon's voice was a hoarse whisper.

If the people on the sidewalk looked, they'd possibly see them. In this moment, Trevor was pretty sure neither of them cared.

"I could stay here and not move, be inside you all night," he whispered back. He'd paused but then pulled out slowly and shoved forward again. He kept going, slow and quiet, fucking Simon—no, not fucking but making love to him—until the people walked by and were out of sight.

Trevor pulled almost all the way out and slammed forward again—

harder this time. The table moved but they followed it. Simon reached down, grabbing his cock that was already hard again.

He fucked his own hand while Trevor made love to him—all that tight heat around him. "You feel so good. I never knew…never knew…" He never knew it could be like this.

"Harder," Simon told him and Trevor obeyed. He slammed in, pulled out, and slammed in again. His balls felt like they could explode, but he wanted to keep going, to hold it off as long as he could.

"Trev…oh, fuck yes. Trevor…" Simon stiffened. His ass squeezed tighter, and Trevor couldn't hold it back anymore. He let go, jumping off the fucking edge. Come spilled out of him, once, twice, three times, as he kept moving inside Simon.

And then, he couldn't move. His body was toast. He dropped forward, giving Simon his weight. Simon shifted, moved Trevor off of him but didn't let go of him, either.

"Thank you…Fuck, I can't…"

"It's okay," Trevor cut him off. "Just take me to bed. Give me a little time to rest, and then it's your turn to do that to me."

***

Simon was on edge the whole next morning. It was a minor surgery compared to the ones he'd performed himself. It wasn't that part of it that worried him.

It was the after. It was the waiting, the wondering, the possibility; but also the doubt that carried more weight than his hope did.

This surgery was a long shot. Being a surgeon took a different level of control than most things. He couldn't responsibly do his job if he had pain in his hand, if he had any altered sensation; because one painful jerk, one twitch of his hand could mean life and death.

"You okay?" Trevor asked him as Simon waited to get taken to the back.

He thought about lying but then admitted, "I'm not sure."

Trevor glanced around, as if he was unsure, but then leaned in and gave Simon a quick kiss. It didn't matter to Simon if anyone had seen. He'd needed it.

"You got this, doc," Trevor told him. "No matter what, we'll figure it out."

Meaning if things worked and Simon could get his career back, Trevor wasn't walking away.

"Dr. Malone? They're ready for you now." A nurse stood waiting for Simon.

"You're incredible. Everything about you. I know you don't see it, but I do." Simon smiled at him. "I'll see you soon." And then he turned and walked away from Trevor.

CHAPTER THIRTY-EIGHT

Heather had been right about the surgery. It hadn't taken long at all. Simon went home the next day with a prescription for pain meds. They spent one night at the beach house before driving back home to Rockford Falls. Simon had a post-op evaluation in a week, and from there they would know a little more about how things went.

Trevor would be lying if he didn't admit things were more strained than before. They'd protected themselves in a bubble, which worked for both of them. Trevor hadn't wanted to be around people, and Simon, either, but it seemed whenever they were—whether it was his family or people Simon knew, they didn't jive the same as when they were alone.

A couple days after arriving home, Trevor's mom stopped by to see how Simon was doing. She was trying to get to know the man who meant so much to her son. Simon didn't always do well with people on a good day, and on that day he'd been in a bad mood because of his hand. A random comment from his mom about her upcoming forty-sixth birthday in a couple weeks, shot Simon's irritability up another level. Apparently the fact that he was twelve years older than Trevor, yet less than ten years younger than Trevor's mom, didn't sit well with him.

But when it was just the two of them, things were incredible. It was more than Trevor ever thought he would have.

Simon asked about Trevor officially moving all his things in, yet Trevor still hadn't done it.

In his life, he'd had made too many mistakes to count. He didn't want this to be another one. He didn't want to jump without thinking things through, even though the thought of sharing a home with Simon was close to irresistible.

But then, he loved Simon. They'd been together for months. They had a great friendship. They made each other happy. Shouldn't that be all that mattered?

Maybe, if it wasn't for the surgery. If Trevor was being honest, that was a big part of it for him. If it worked, Simon would want to go back to the city. Trevor knew himself well enough to admit he had no business in San Francisco for anything longer than a few days at a time. The city was too alive. The temptation was too great. He had to be smart, but he also didn't think he could give this up.

"You've been quiet lately. That's not like a Dixon brother." Jase nudged him as they stood, drinking water. The sun burned down on them. Summer was coming to an end, and Trevor couldn't wait for it.

"Did you love Blake?" he asked out of the blue. He'd never really talked to either of them about their relationship before. He'd been too fucked up to care. Plus, before he knew what it felt like, thoughts of love were never really on his radar.

"This about the doctor?" Jason poured the rest of his water over his head, wetting his short, blond hair.

Trevor rolled his eyes. "No, I've always been interested in your love life with my brother."

"Oh, I see. You think you're funny now?" Jason teased.

Trevor shook his head. "Yeah, it's about Simon."

Jason sat down on the curb, and Trevor joined him. Blake was still inside working. "I don't think so. I mean, I love him. He's a good friend, but I don't think I was ever *in* love with him. I think it was more just something that happened. We were friends. We were both gay. We were both dealing with heavy shit that we didn't want to deal with. Being with each other helped mask it. Being with each other every once in a while still helps." He nudged Trevor's arm and laughed.

Trevor ignored him. He really didn't want to discuss his brother's sex life. Trevor also didn't want to get into the heavy shit Jason said Blake had been dealing with back then because he knew it was probably him.

"I think maybe there was a time when we wondered if we were in love with each other. It would be easy together. We know each other, we get each other, we both still like each other regardless of knowing one another so well. That's a big one. But I don't think it's love in that sense. We know we always have each other there. It's good to have that. You in love with the doctor?"

Trevor nodded. "Yeah."

"He in love with you?"

That was the part Trevor wasn't sure of. He thought so, but he couldn't say for sure. Simon hadn't said he was. "Don't know."

They were silent for a few minutes. Cars drove past them and Jason picked at the wrapper on his water bottle until they heard Blake call, "Trev! Jase! I need you guys for a minute!" from inside the building.

Trevor went to stand but before he could, Jason laid a hand on his knee. "He's proud of you, ya know? Even if he doesn't admit it. We all are. You're doing real good."

Trevor paused, and let those words sink in. "Thank you," he said, meaning it. It was something he needed to hear. Something he really hoped like hell he'd keep hearing.

***

People always said doctors made the worst patients, Simon would agree. He wasn't supposed to be driving, but since he skipped his pain pill, he decided it was okay to make a trip to the grocery store. Trevor would be home (the home he still hadn't agreed to move in to) from work soon, and they needed some food in the house. Easy food, mind you, but food all the same.

He only made it down a few aisles before he saw someone familiar a few feet in front of him. She had her back to him. It made him a coward, but Simon knew he could back out of the aisle and she would never know he was there.

But he couldn't do that. He'd already made an ass of himself in front of her, not once but twice. If he wanted Trevor to move in with him, learning to be around his family was probably pretty important. "Tiffany?"

Trevor's mom turned to look at him with a cautious smile. Eight years. Trevor's mother was only around eight years older than he was. She'd been twenty when she had Trevor. He was closer in age to Tiffany than he was her son.

Maybe it shouldn't make him uncomfortable, but it did. Uncomfortable wasn't the right word, he didn't think. Unsure? Did Tiffany think he was too old for her son? If he was being honest, he would admit that probably wasn't her first worry when it came to him. She more likely thought he was too big of an asshole for her son.

"Hey, Simon. How are you?" She shifted nervously. He couldn't blame her for that. He probably wouldn't want to be around himself either if he were her.

"I'm okay. Recovering. We'll know more soon."

"I've been sending good thoughts your way. Trevor's told me what you lost…what you're hoping to get back. He knows how important this is to you. We're all pulling for you."

Simon knew that Trevor did. It didn't surprise him that his lover had shared those things with her. He was like that. He didn't struggle with his feelings the way Simon did. And…it meant something that Tiffany wanted this for Simon as well. It came from her need to see her son happy. For her, Simon being happy would help make Trevor happy. But still, he felt a strange twist in his chest that she'd thought about him.

She loved her son. Just looking at her, that was obvious. She wasn't sure how she felt about Simon. He could see that as well, but she tried because Trevor meant so much to her. He was glad his lover had that. And he wanted her to know that her son meant a lot to him as well. "I care about him. I know that I haven't made the best impression, but I want you to know he's important to me. His happiness and well-being are both important to me."

This time, the smile she gave him was genuine. "Thank you. I think I needed to hear that, Simon. Trevor…he's happy. I haven't seen him happy in a long time. Too long, and he deserves it. He's been through more than any man his age should have to go through."

A warmth spread though him, a contentment. He wanted that. Not just for Trevor to be happy, but for Trevor to be happy with him. "He has. I'm proud of him. I respect him greatly for the man he is. That says something about you as well. You raised a fine son."

A man who made Simon happy, too.

"Thank you." Tiffany reached over and grabbed his left hand, and gave it a gentle squeeze. "Thank you," she said again.

CHAPTER THIRTY-NINE

Simon was at the store when Trevor came in after work. He'd kick his ass for that. Trevor could have stopped on the way home, but he'd beaten Trevor to the punch.

Simon had given him a key to the guesthouse. He hadn't moved in yet. He didn't have the furniture to fill it yet, and things were too hectic because of his hand. Trevor knew he would have to give Simon a real answer soon. And he wanted to. He did, even if he was still nervous about it.

Trevor jumped into the shower, and cleaned off all the dirt and sweat from his day. When he got out, he wrapped a towel around his waist before reaching for his razor where it usually sat on the counter, and it wasn't there.

Simon had been a little antsy. He stayed home half the time anyway, but since having the surgery, he felt like he was going crazy. He'd been cleaning (left handed) like mad for a few days now.

Trevor kneeled and opened the cabinet under the sink to see if his razor was there. He pushed a few things aside. A bottle of peroxide fell over, and he picked it up.

His eyes darted to the left of the bottle and…

It wasn't the razor that caught his attention, though.

A bottle.

A bottle Simon had tried to hide from Trevor. He'd been very quiet about taking his pain medication since his surgery.

The bottle drew his attention again.

Oxycodone.

Oxy, oxy, oxy, oxy.

He'd had some fun on oxy.

Trevor slammed the cabinet shut. Took a few deep breaths. Closed his eyes, rubbed them, as though he could unsee the pills there. As though he could forget. He couldn't. He could still see them even with the cabinet door closed.

Move, he instructed his legs. *Fucking move. Stand up. Walk away. Do something.*

But it didn't work. He started to sweat. His vision blurred, so he rubbed his eyes again,, trying to clear them, but that made it even worse. His vision zeroed in on the cabinet.

Then a part of him did move, but not his legs. His arm. His hand. Trevor opened the cabinet again. Grabbed the bottle before falling backward to sit against the wall.

It had been so long. He shouldn't still want it this bad. Why did he still want it this bad?

Just one. He could take one and Simon would never know. One pill wouldn't do much to him…just take the edge off. Help him forget about his worries with his brother, help him forget the pain he'd caused his mother. His fear over how he felt about Simon, and maybe clear his head so his decision became a little easier.

Trevor touched the white lid. Almost twisted it, but then threw it back into the cabinet. He slammed the door closed.

He should go to a meeting. Call his sponsor. He knew that. But instead he grabbed his coin, climbed into the bed, and lay on his side.

Trevor hated that he still wanted it. Hated that time didn't seem to ease it. Not when he had a bottle of oxy waiting for him in the other room.

And then he thought of Simon. He'd had to hide his fucking pills under the cabinet because Trevor was so weak. Because he was scared whether Trevor could handle it or not. And apparently he had a good reason to feel that way. How could he bring all his demons into Simon's home? How could he ask Simon to deal with him, all day, every day?

The answer was, he couldn't.

***

The house was quiet when Simon got home. He set the bags of groceries on the counter, and then went for the bedroom. "Trev? Are you in the shower?" He turned into the room to see Trevor lying down, with his back to Simon, in nothing except a towel.

The hairs on the back of his neck stood.

Something was wrong. He could see it in the set of his lover's body.

In the fact that he didn't turn to look at Simon.

Simon's heart sped up. "Are you feeling okay?" He walked toward the bed, stopped so close that his legs were touching it before Trevor spoke.

"I can't do this. I'm scared of fucking up."

Simon's chest hurt his heart beat so hard. Nausea twisted his stomach, tied it into knots. *Please don't let him have relapsed.* "Hey. You're doing great. You're not going to screw up." Simon's voice shook.

Had he already taken something? Was he coming down? High? Simon wanted to ask, but he wanted to believe in Trevor, too. Because Trevor needed that, needed someone who believed in him. "It's a process. You've been clean for over a year. That's incredible. You have every right to be proud of yourself. *I'm* proud of you." Simon walked around to the other side of the bed and looked down at Trevor. It broke his heart to see the man like that. He was shaking. Scared. Hurt.

"I've never had as much respect for anyone in my life as I have for you. It would be so easy for you to give in, but you don't. You fight. You made me want to fight. That's why I had the surgery. I fought because of you." And that was the truth.

"I almost took one of your pills a few minutes ago. I sat on the floor and held the bottle in my hand. It took everything inside of me not to take one, or hell, more than one."

Simon closed his eyes. Fuck. That was on him. He shouldn't have even kept them in the house. "But you didn't. That's what matters. You didn't. I see that as a success, Trev. Nothing more."

Simon moved slowly. He crawled over Trevor and tucked himself in behind him. Wrapped an arm around his waist, the front of his body molded to the back of Trevor's.

And he knew right then that he loved the man. No question. He would do anything for him. Seeing him hurt like this broke Simon. He wanted to fix it. Would do whatever he could to make it go away.

His mouth was close to Trevor's ear when he whispered, "You're strong. You can do this. You're doing it. And I'm right here every step of the way."

Trevor didn't reply, and Simon didn't move. He just held him. Wanted Trevor to know he was there.

"We can go to a meeting. I'll go with you, or you can go alone. If you want me to call someone, I can do that too. What do you need?" He was so out of his element here. He'd never dealt with this. "What do you need, Trev? Whatever it is, I'll give it to you."

Trevor rolled over, and on top of Simon. "I just want to be okay. I want to forget about everything else. I just want you."

And then his lips came down on Simon's. Simon opened for him, let Trevor's tongue invade his mouth.

This was probably wrong. The wrong thing to do at the wrong time, but he couldn't say no…because Trevor needed him, and he needed Trevor right now too. Needed to feel close to him, because seeing Trevor broken like this rocked Simon to his core.

Trevor was the strong one between them. He knew that, and it did something to his insides, something he'd never experienced to see Trevor so lost.

He needed Trevor back, wanted to pull him away from the edge and hold him. Keep him safe.

He would do anything for him.

Simon was in love with him.

CHAPTER FORTY

Trevor didn't stop kissing Simon. He wanted his mouth on him, his tongue in him, until he forgot who he was. Forgot that he was the man who, moments ago, sat shaking on the bathroom floor because he wanted a stupid fucking pill so badly. He wanted to be in a place where nothing existed except the way Simon made him feel.

They always had this, the bed, where it didn't matter who they were. Where it didn't matter that Trevor was recovering, or that Simon was older or a doctor, or any of the other differences they had between them.

And Trevor needed to hold onto that.

Simon wrapped his arms around Trevor's waist, squeezed him tightly, and Trevor kept kissing. Kept himself familiar with every inch of Simon's mouth.

But he wanted more, needed more. Needed friction and skin on skin. Wanted them to sweat together, to come together. So he slid down Simon's body. Trevor pushed his shirt up until it reached Simon's chest. He could take it from there.

And he did. As Trevor took care of Simon's jeans, he pulled his shirt over his head and tossed it.

That's what he wanted. Skin. Something good, not the mess he'd just been. He ran his tongue from Simon's balls to the tip of his erection. He tasted slightly salty, the way Trevor liked. He let out a hiss when Trevor sucked the crown and then groaned when Trevor let it pop out of his mouth again.

"Give me your mouth." Simon told him.

"That's what I'm doing." He lay on Simon again. Their dicks rubbed together as Trevor rut against him, kissing Simon again. Jesus, sober sex was so much better. He hadn't realized before how much he loved just kissing, touching, rubbing off on each other. His cock slid between Simon's crotch and leg, before rubbing against his shaft again.

Simon's palms tried to cup his ass, to pull him closer, but Trevor could tell it was hard with his hand. He felt the tape and bandages rubbing his skin.

He kissed Simon's neck. "Don't. You'll hurt yourself."

"I don't really care right now."

But he did. Trevor knew he did, so he grabbed Simon's right arm and pulled it over Simon's head. "Yes, you do. And I care too."

Trevor pushed up, using his forearms to hold himself up so he could see the space between them. See his dick meet Simon's as they thrust against each other.

He wanted this. Fuck, he only wanted a normal life. To work, and come home and make love to Simon every night without having to stress about meetings and sobriety. But that wasn't what he had. It wasn't Trevor's reality.

"I already want to come. Want you inside me." And then when they recovered, he wanted to fuck Simon all night so he could forget about everything else.

Trevor reached for the condoms and lube. He squirted some on Simon's left hand as he straddled Simon, chest-to-chest. He kissed Simon's neck, his chest, let their pricks slide together as Simon worked a lubed finger inside him.

There wasn't a lot of preparation because a finger wasn't enough and Trevor wasn't the best at waiting. He wanted Simon now, so he pulled away. Ripped open a condom wrapper and rolled it down Simon's thick erection.

Enough waiting. Trevor sat up, held himself up on his knees as he reached behind himself, guided Simon's cock to his hole, and slowly lowered himself down.

***

Jesus Christ, that felt good. Trevor's tight ass, all that heat squeezing him so fucking tightly. Trevor rose, and then sat again, then again, riding Simon's cock. Each time Trevor lowered, Simon pumped, slamming into Trevor.

He wanted to come.

He never wanted to stop.

He wanted this. Trevor. Baggage and all. Nothing else mattered to Simon. Trevor was his.

He wrapped a hand around Trevor's erection. Pumped three times before he exploded, erupted, thick white stripes of come shooting up Simon's chest. Trevor's asshole clenched, tightened around Simon's prick. He squeezed Trevor's sides. Pain shot through his hand but he didn't care. Not right now. He came so hard his vision went blurry, and then he pulled Trevor down, fusing their mouths together.

Trevor held the condom in place as he pulled off, then took the condom and tossed it into the trash. Simon grabbed him, pulled him close, as they both lay on their sides the way they had when Simon first got into bed with him.

"I didn't take it," Trevor finally said.

"I know." They'd gone over it before, but he knew Trevor needed to say it again, and he needed Simon to believe him. "We'll do whatever you need to do. If this is too much, we'll slow down. If you need more meetings, you'll go to them. Whatever you need. I'm not walking away." Which was a big step for Simon. He'd been known for walking away. He'd done it with Heather. He'd even done it when his hand got injured.

Trevor still had his back to Simon when he spoke. "You fight, too, baby. You do. You just did, and when you're performing surgery again, you'll know it's because you didn't give up."

Simon's chest ached at those words.

"I want that for you. You deserve it. Maybe it's wrong of me to think about it this way, but I don't see where I have a place in that. You deserve to be in San Francisco like you were. It's hard for me here, but I have support. I don't know if I could do it there."

Simon squeezed Trevor tighter. Wishing neither of them had to deal with all of this shit. Part of him wanting exactly what Trevor said, to have the mobility in his hand back and to be in San Francisco again, but the other part, just wanted to be here with Trevor.

Why did things have to be so black or white? If this worked, it wasn't as though it was impossible for Simon to work here…though it wouldn't be the same. But being without Trevor? He didn't think he could do that, either.

"I dream about it sometimes. The feeling of the bat shattering my hand, taking away everything I ever wanted…and I hate it. It's amazing how one little thing can change your life. It was the warmest day we'd had in weeks, and I left the front door open to get air. I should have closed the door. Having it open made me an easy mark. If I hadn't had it open, would he have chosen a different house? If I hadn't been gripping something when he hit me, things could have been different. It wouldn't have put the same pressure on the nerves. My life could have gone on the way it was. I want to kill the man who did it. I would kill him with my bare hands if I could." Another truth filled Simon's head in that moment. "But sometimes…I look around at this property. My home…you…and maybe this is how things are supposed to be. Maybe that's why everything happened. Maybe it was all to get me here."

"No. Fuck that. I saw you, Simon. I know what you want."

He did, but he wanted this too. "I couldn't even tell the police what he looked like. I heard a noise, turned, he swung, and on reflex my hand when up to protect me. I happened to be holding a bottle in my hand. Nothing else mattered. It didn't matter that everything else about that day had been normal. March thirteenth, the same as any other day…"

Trevor's body stiffened, turned cold, and then he shot out of the bed. "What did you say?"

Simon sat up, heart racing. "It was the thirteenth of March. Why? What's wrong?"

Trevor went pale. His whole body visibly went weak. He reached out, and leaned a hand on the wall to hold himself up. "Where? Where the fuck did it happen, Simon? Where did you live?"

"Outside of San Francisco. Middle of nowhere, really. Out on Route 241."

Trevor backed farther away from Simon. He probably realized it right then but couldn't admit it. His whole body started to ache. The pain began in his chest, in his heart, and echoed out until it took over every part of Simon's body. "Come back to bed." He didn't want to hear it. Didn't want to hear anything. Simon couldn't let himself believe it. "Come back to bed, Trevor."

But he didn't. He only shook his head, closed his eyes. When he opened them again, they looked frantic. "You had the door open…I saw the door open… The front of your house was mostly all windows, wasn't it? With a huge deck out front."

"Trevor." No. Fuck no. This couldn't be happening.

"Tell me!" he yelled. "Tell me I'm wrong!"

That's when he knew. The clues had been there, hadn't they? Trevor had been sober about as long as it had been since Simon's injury. It had happened outside of the city. Trevor had been partying in the city before waking up in a car in the middle of nowhere. He'd seen his friend walk into a house…

Trevor only stopped backing away when he hit the far wall. "It was me. I could have stopped him. I got drunk and high with a man, drove in a car with him. We could have killed someone. I saw him walk into a house. I could have gone in, tried to stop him, but I didn't. Instead I stumbled out of the car, got lost in the woods and almost choked on my own vomit. He ruined your whole fucking life, and I could have stopped him!" Trevor shook his head. Simon's stomach ached more with each second. He felt like he could vomit. He just wanted Trevor to shut up, but he kept speaking. "I said earlier that I figured he was going somewhere to party, but I knew, on some level I knew he was robbing someone or something. What the fuck would he be doing at a house like that? We didn't spend time with people who lived in houses like that. It's why I stumbled away, so I wouldn't be involved. I *knew* and I didn't do a God Damned thing!"

Jesus Christ. The man he hated, the man who ruined his career, took Simon's identity away from him, had been with Trevor. Trevor had seen him walk into Simon's house, and had done nothing to stop it. Trevor had partied with him and fucked him before he let the man ruin Simon's life. "You didn't know." Simon shook his head, not wanting to believe it. That's what he had to focus on, the fact that Trevor didn't know.

He looked up just as Trevor grabbed a pair of white sweats, and pulled them on. He leaned against the wall, still letting it hold him up. "Does that really matter, though? I still did nothing. All I had to do was call his name. Walk in and everything could have been different."

And maybe Simon would still have his life. He would still be the man he'd always wanted to be.

Simon couldn't move. Couldn't think. Trevor was tied to what happened to his hand. The man he loved was a part of what had taken away the most important thing in his life.

The man I love... But that didn't even matter right now. It couldn't. He didn't know if he could get past this. If he had it in him to forget.

Trevor looked down, a sad smile on his face. "I knew it would be me who fucked this up. I'm sorry, baby. I love you." Trevor grabbed a shirt. He didn't say another word as he walked out…and Simon did nothing to stop him.

CHAPTER FORTY-ONE

Trevor felt like his head was spinning. His gut cramped. He was splitting apart from the inside out. He was cracking, breaking, disintegrating.

There were a hundred things he could have done differently that day that could have changed Simon's life. Not been on so many drugs. Getting out of the car. Stopping Greg.

Would he really have, though? He didn't know. Back then he only cared about getting fucked up, if he thought there was something in Simon's house he could use or sell, would he have stopped Greg? *Please. Please tell me I would have stopped him.*

Trevor leaned against his truck in front of Simon's house. He couldn't hold back the vomit as it crawled up his throat. His stomach aced as he emptied it in Simon's driveway. He'd done so much shit, too much shit to remember it all.

He couldn't say if he would have stopped Greg.

He was there, sitting in the car when Simon was getting attacked.

He'd walked away, gotten lost, while Simon went to the hospital, while they told Simon how badly his hand had been damaged.

That he couldn't operate again.

Simon saved lives.

Trevor fucked them up.

And he'd been a part of what had taken that away from Simon.

This whole time he thought as long as he kept on track, as long as he worked toward being a better man, everything would be okay. But it wouldn't. Maybe he didn't deserve for it to be okay, either. Maybe he'd gone too far, done too much, and it was only a matter of time until he hurt someone again.

He'd hurt more people than he'd ever realized.

Trevor jumped into his truck and drove away.

***

Simon didn't move from his bed. He couldn't. Their conversation replayed through his mind. Trevor's admission, when he realized what was going on, the fear and shame in Trevor's voice… The truth, the part he struggled to swallow, kept repeating in his head. *Trevor was there, Trevor was there, Trevor was there.*

He'd been drunk and high in front of Simon's house while he watched his friend, the man he'd recently fucked, walk into Simon's house.

And Trevor had left... disappeared, while the man had taken away the only thing Simon had ever loved.

But no…that wasn't true, either. He'd loved his dad. He loved Heather. He loved Trevor.

But he didn't know if he could forgive him. Simon shoved out of bed, but didn't make it far. He slid to the ground, back against the bed, staring at his hand. The hand that he would probably never be able to use in surgery again.

No, right or wrong, he didn't know if he could ever forgive Trevor for that.

But he did love him. And he didn't want Trevor hurt. The thought of Trevor in pain rocked through him, a heavy anchor in his gut, weighing him down.

Simon's hand shook as he grabbed his cell. Dialed. The phone rang before going to Trevor's voicemail.

He hung up, and called again. And again. No answer. The anchor got heavier, the worry thicker with each call. The third time the voicemail picked up, he finally spoke. "Don't…don't do anything you'll regret. Just…" Just what? Come back? Simon couldn't ask him to come back. Not now, and maybe not ever, but he couldn't handle thinking Trevor might risk everything he'd accomplished. The new life that meant so much to him. Trevor couldn't relapse. Not after all this time. "Please, don't do it. I really need you to be okay. Do you hear me, Trev? I need you to be okay. Your family needs you. Don't do anything."

Regardless of it all, Simon needed Trevor to be okay.

"Please," he added again, and then he hung up the phone, before dialing again.

Blake answered on the second ring, "Rock Solid, this is Blake."

"It's Simon. I—"

"What's wrong? Where's Trev?"

He knew. That quickly, he knew. Simon closed his eyes at the pain in Blake's voice. He felt the same ache inside himself. Knowing what happened would kill Trevor. Simon knew that. "He left. I'm worried about him. We have to find him."

"I'll be right there," Blake said and hung up the phone.

Simon got dressed and went outside. He was pacing the porch when Blake pulled up five minutes later.

"What happened?" Blake slammed the door of his truck, and the pain in Simon's chest intensified. It felt like a betrayal in a way—both calling Blake and not believing in Trevor. But then, he'd rather be cautious, rather worry about Trevor than risk not doing what the man needed. Regardless, he would need his family.

"I don't think he'll use. I…he's been doing so well. He wants to be sober. I see it in him every day, the determination. He wants this. He could have taken my pain pills and he didn't."

"You left them where he could get to them?" Blake bellowed. A vein pulsed in his forehead. He wanted to hit Simon. The way his hands fisted proved that.

"Yes. I fucked up. But Trevor didn't. He didn't take them. Can we not waste time with this shit? I need to know where he would go. If he's upset, or hurt, or angry, where would he go?" He didn't know. Simon should know that. Those were the kinds of things you found out about someone you loved. Why didn't Simon try to find out more about him?

Blake's eyes darkened. They were so close to the same color as Trevor's, they looked almost identical, but they were different, too. His weren't lighter close to the pupil, like Trevor's. They didn't make Simon feel the way that Trevor's did.

"What happened?" Blake asked again.

"I failed him." Regardless of what they discovered, he should have made sure Trevor was okay. That was more important than anything else. "I let him go when I shouldn't have. Help me." The words felt so foreign on his tongue. He squeezed his fist so tightly, the nails on Simon's left hand dug into his palm. Had he ever asked for help before? No matter how hard things got—when he wanted his dad to spend time with him so badly, with Heather or anyone else in his life, he'd never asked for help. It was worth it for Trevor. "Help me," he begged. "Help me find him."

Blake paused, his eyes firmly on Simon. Blake didn't move as he studied Simon, studied him in a way he'd never done before. The anger that he usually had when he looked at Simon wasn't there anymore. It was almost as if he finally trusted Simon, just when it might be too late. "We'll find him. He'll be okay. I promise you, we'll find him."

CHAPTER FORTY-TWO

It felt as though Trevor just closed his eyes, and when he opened them again, he was in San Francisco. He didn't remember driving here, didn't remember making the choice to come, but he had to have, because he was here.

It was different than when he'd come with Simon. Even though he had ghosts hiding in the corners, just as many here as he had back home, and even though he'd been nervous and uncomfortable coming back, he almost felt resigned this time. With Simon, those ghosts hadn't shined so brightly. They'd stay hidden, whispering for Trevor to find them rather than the loud voices in his brain, yelling for his attention this time.

He'd just been biding his time, really. It wasn't like he would be able to stay clean forever. Not him. He'd liked it too much. The high was too exciting, too much fun. Life? Responsibility? Trying so damn hard? What did that get him? He would always be the same Trevor. There was no changing that, no matter how much he wanted to be someone else. No matter how much he wanted to be the guy Blake could depend on, who didn't break his own mother's heart on a regular basis, and the kind of man who deserved Simon, that would never be Trevor. Not after all he'd done. What was the purpose of continuing to fight it?

No. He shook his head. He couldn't do this. He wouldn't. Trevor refused to throw away his new life. He fought to drown out the devil in his head with everything that meant something to him, everything good in his life: *Mom, Blake, Rock Solid, Simon...*

The thought of letting them down made another wave of nausea hit him, but there was nothing left in his stomach to lose. He'd left everything back at Simon's. Maybe he'd even left the Trevor he'd tried to become in Rockford Falls as well.

Trevor rubbed his eyes with the palms of his hands, trying to take away the vision of Simon's house, of seeing Greg at the door and doing nothing. Of getting out of the car and walking away. Of the pain in Simon's eyes every time he spoke about surgery, and how it intensified when he realized Trevor was connected to it. When he realized what everyone else knew already about Trevor—that eventually he would let everyone down.

Just once... One more time, to help take the edge off. To help get through...

He knew exactly where to go.

***

Twenty-four hours passed since Trevor walked out of Simon's house. His phone started going straight to voicemail a long time ago. Either it died, or he'd turned it off.

Blake led Simon through all the places Trevor used to go in Rockford Falls. When they couldn't find him there, they went to San

Francisco.

Unfortunately, Blake wasn't as familiar with Trevor's old stomping grounds in the city, so they basically drove around and hoped to get lucky.

They hadn't.

Each second that went by, the heavier the anchor in Simon's gut got. The more the ache in his chest intensified. It was like something inside him was breaking, breaking in a way he'd never known. He needed to find Trevor.

Simon should have known better. No matter how he felt when he found out, he should have made sure Trevor was okay. That's what a person did when they loved someone. They put them first. Simon had never done that in his life. He wasn't sure he knew how.

Blake's voice from the passenger seat snapped Simon out of his thoughts. "I always looked up to my brother. It's funny, because we're twins, we're alike in so many ways, but I always wanted to be more like him. There's something about Trevor people love. They want to be around him. He makes them feel good. Makes them laugh. I've never had that." Blake faced the window, looking out. Funny, Simon knew that's how Trevor felt about Blake.

"I can see that. I feel that way about him. I've respected him since the first day I met him. I could tell it was a struggle for him, but he didn't take the medication. The next day, it was stupid of him to come to my house, irresponsible in some ways, but I'd admired him for that too. He didn't give up." Simon could only hope Trevor didn't give up now, either. "Most people aren't that strong. I'm not that strong." And he wasn't. He'd given up. When he realized his hand would never be the same, he'd folded. It was all or nothing. Simon had always been that way. He didn't move on with this life the way Trevor did when he got sober.

"He's stubborn as hell." Blake laughed, but Simon couldn't make himself do the same.

"I spent too much time feeling sorry for myself after I got hurt. Jesus, I have more than most people, but I couldn't see it. I didn't want to. He made me want to. He makes me feel like things would be okay, regardless." He made Simon feel and do a lot of things he hadn't felt in a long time, if ever.

"It means everything to him not to let you down anymore. You or your mom. You're a family, and that means the world to Trevor. I've never had that. He's okay. I have to believe he's okay." Simon's left thumb drummed on the steering wheel.

"You're in love with him," Blake said. "Does he know?"

"I never told him." Because that was Simon; it was easier to keep things in. Easier not to feel. To put everything else over his emotions. So, he hadn't put himself out there. Not in the realest way he could. Maybe if he had, they wouldn't be here right now.

"He loves you. Trevor doesn't love easily, but he loves you. He knows you feel the same."

Christ, those words somehow managed to ease some of the ache in Simon's chest. He needed Trevor to know how he felt. He needed to hear again that Trevor loved him. Simon glanced over at Blake, the truth on his tongue. "He was there. He didn't know what was happening, but he was with the man who injured my hand. Trevor left, and we didn't realize the connection until yesterday. It was in his final binge before he went to rehab."

The air in the car suddenly rose fifty degrees. It was so thick, Simon felt like he would choke on it.

"Shit," Blake finally mumbled after what felt like an eternity. "That's going to wreck him."

"I know."

"Can you get past it?"

Unfortunately, Simon wasn't sure he had an answer for that.

CHAPTER FORTY-THREE

Trevor sat alone, lights out, in his dark hotel room. His cell phone was dead beside him. The battery had been low when he left Simon's, and he hadn't charged it.

He needed to call his brother and let Blake know he was okay. Even if Simon hadn't called him (he knew Simon well enough to know he would), Blake would be worried about him by now. Even when Trevor didn't go home, he called. At least now he did. He'd never bothered before he got sober.

It was selfish of him not to do so right now.

Trevor reached over, felt the bottle on the nightstand as though it had somehow disappeared. It was cold against his skin. Welcoming. Familiar. A long lost friend that he'd missed. A lover who had comforted him when he needed it. Someone he had lost but now found again.

It would be the easiest thing in the world to do, to open it. To take a drink. Relapsing would be a whole hell of a lot easier than staying sober. Relapsing meant he could forget, stop feeling, stop remembering. Stop caring.

Trevor wrapped his fingers around it again. Held it before lifting it off the table and into his lap. He clicked the lamp on the bedside table. He looked at the tray, eying each object—the spoon, the baggie, the lighter, the needle. His eyes went back to the heroin again.

The bottle was the lesser of the two evils. People drank every day. Blake did. Simon did. He could handle just that—take a drink and continue to live his life. It was a normal part of life.

It had never been that easy for Trevor, though. It likely never would, and he wasn't sure he had the strength to fight it anymore.

***

The next morning Simon sat in one of the spare bedrooms at Heather's house. Blake had gone home the night before. They had no evidence that Trevor had even come here. If he was missing much longer, they could contact the police, but Simon wasn't sure it would do any good. He was a grown man who'd walked out on his lover and had a history of drug abuse. They had some time before Trevor missing would be taken seriously.

He'd just gotten dressed, ready to go out and spend the day driving around the city and calling Trevor again, when his phone rang. His heart sped up, pounding against his chest, a mixture of fear and hope. It was the same emotions he felt every time he performed a surgery—fear that he wasn't enough, but hope that he was.

He didn't recognize the number. "Hello?"

"I'm sorry…I'm sorry…I'm sorry…" Trevor continued to repeat over and over through the line. His voice was low, sorrow pouring out of every, "I'm so sorry."

"Where are you, Trev? Are you okay?"

"I'm sorry," he said again.

"It's okay." No matter what happened, it would be okay. Simon would make sure of it. He wouldn't walk away.

"I shouldn't have called you. It's wrong. Not after everything, but I need your help. I—" Trevor's voice broke. "Fuck, why do I always screw up?"

His body shook. His muscles tight. "Yes, you should have called me, Trev. Only me. Always me." As soon as the words were out, Simon realized how true they were. Whatever happened, whatever Trevor needed, Simon wanted to be there for him. In that moment, hearing the broken voice of the man he loved, having it settle inside every part of him, he realized he would do anything to make things okay—including forgiving him for being there that day. He needed Trevor healthy. Simon needed Trevor with him more than he needed his hand to heal, or to ever fix a heart again. Because without Trevor, Simon's heart would always be broken. Trevor was the only one with the power to fix Simon's.

Nothing else mattered. Simon needed Trevor to have a future.

"We'll get through it. Whatever it is, we'll get through it, Trev. I'm not leaving you. Tell me where you are."

There was a pause before Trevor replied, "Room 201. The Hotel by the Bay… I need you to come and get me, and take me to rehab."

Simon's pulse dropped, stopped, but he meant what he said. "We'll get through it. Stay on the phone with me, okay? I'm on my way."

CHAPTER FORTY-FOUR

Trevor couldn't stop shaking. His whole body trembled uncontrollably. His heart beat faster than it ever had in his life. So fast he thought it might explode.

There was a knock on the door fifteen minutes later. Each minute had felt like twenty. He hated this. Hated that he had to call Simon, that Simon had to see him this way, but there was no one else he wanted to do this with. Just Simon. His legs were weak as he walked to the door. Trevor pulled it open, and then Simon was there, holding Trevor to his chest and saying, "I'm sorry."

"You have nothing to be sorry for. It was me." He'd been with Greg. He'd been weak, and walked out on Simon.

"I could have handled it better. I should have made sure you knew I was there for you."

Trevor shook his head and pulled back, needing to take responsibility for himself. "I have to be able to deal. I have to be able to handle things on my own. If I can't, then what kind of life do I have? I have to take responsibility, Simon. Of what happened to you, and what

I've let my life become. I can't blame other people." Simon closed the door, but didn't come closer.

In that part, Blake and his mom had been right. Trevor wasn't ready for a relationship if he was going to break the second it got hard. "Maybe it was too soon."

"No." Simon said. "Not for me, and I don't think so for you, either." Simon stepped forward, cupped Trevor's cheek, and Trevor wanted to live there, in that moment. He wanted everything else to drop away—but it couldn't. Life didn't work that way. He had to take the bad and the good. Everyone did.

"It wasn't your fault."

Trevor closed his eyes. "I have to take some responsibility. I can't say I played no part." Before getting sober, he'd spent years doing that, not taking responsibility for his own life.

Trevor pulled back, watched Simon's hand drop away and then went toward the bed. "I need to get rid of the stuff. I needed someone here with me when I did it. Then we can go."

He felt Simon behind him. Shame burrowed into every crevice of Trevor at the things Simon saw—an open bottle of whiskey—but still full. Not one single drink taken from it. Heroin, a needle…

"You didn't take it?" Simon's voice sounded far away even though he was close.

"No. None of it. But I bought it. I almost took it. It took everything inside of me not to."

"But you didn't. You're here, and you called me. Give yourself some credit, Trevor. You don't know all of the things you're capable of. What you've accomplished. What you give your family. What you give me. You think you took my life from me, too, but you didn't...you gave me one."

Those words were everything to him. He needed to hear them, needed to believe them. Because he loved Simon... loved him with all he had. And he wanted to be able to love himself too.

Simon started, "I—"

"Don't," Trevor cut him off. "Not yet. Let's not do this yet." Whether Simon knew it or not, he needed time. They both did.

Simon seemed to understand. He watched, standing close to Trevor as Trevor dumped the whiskey down the sink. He didn't leave when Trevor flushed the heroin down the toilet.

And it felt good. Not just that Simon was there, but that he'd done it. That he hadn't taken the drugs. That he'd asked for help. He could do this. He would become the man he always wanted to be.

***

They were silent almost the whole way to the rehab facility. Simon kept his hand on Trevor's leg the entire time, letting Trevor know he was there for him. And he would be. Simon wasn't walking away. Not from this man.

Since he hadn't taken the drugs, Trevor didn't have to do this, but Simon respected the hell out of him that he was. He hadn't used. He'd come close, but he hadn't, yet he took his sobriety seriously enough that he decided to come here again.

Simon pulled into the circular driveway in front of the building. It looked nice, the kind of place Simon would want for him. "I'm so damned proud of you," he told Trevor. "You're a stronger man than I've ever been." His hand felt like nothing now. He couldn't perform surgery? So what. He could still be a doctor. He still had a life. People dealt with things worse than Simon. He was done feeling sorry for himself.

He just wanted to live.

A woman stepped out of the building, shaded by an awning over the porch. She smiled, holding a folder in her hand. There was a fountain off to the side of the white building. Trees and flowers were everywhere.

"You'll call Blake?" Trevor asked.

"The second I leave."

"Shit. The business. I'm screwing him over."

Simon squeezed Trevor's leg. "He loves you. That's all that matters. We'll figure it out." We. Because Simon was a part of this now. "I brought something for you." Simon reached into his pocket and pulled out Trevor's one year sober coin. "You left it at home."

"I…" Trevor squeezed his eyes closed, and Simon could see how much this meant to him. "Keep it for me."

"It's yours. You earned this," Simon told him.

"I want you to have it. I have to go." Trevor opened the door and got out. Simon couldn't stop himself from doing the same.

He met Trevor on the other side of the car before he could walk away and pulled him into a hug. "I love you," he whispered in Trevor's ear. Fuck waiting. He wanted to make sure Trevor knew now. He'd done enough keeping quiet, enough holding his emotions inside. "No matter what, I love you and I'm here. I'll be waiting for you."

Trevor tensed up and then relaxed against him. "Yeah?" he asked.

"Yeah. No matter how long it takes. And if you aren't ready when you get out, I'll still be waiting for when you are."

His whole life he'd never felt like he had anyone to love. No family, just his studies. Then he met Heather, and as great as she was, for him, she wasn't it. He knew love now. Knew what was important, what he needed and who he was. He was Dr. Simon Malone, and Trevor was all he needed.

Trevor's hand tightened in Simon's shirt as he squeezed him tighter. "I have to go."

And then he pulled back. Simon watched until he got almost to the porch, stopped, and turned to him. "I love you, too. Pick me up in thirty days?"

Simon smiled. "I'll be here."

EPILOGUE

One year later

"Trevor! Simon! Can one of you help me? My hands are full."

Trevor stepped into the living room to help his mom, just as Simon made it to her. "I got it." After taking a couple of the bags from her, Simon leaned forward and kissed her cheek. "We're glad you could make it."

"Pfft." She swatted his arm. "Like I would miss it."

Trevor enjoyed watching Simon with her. They'd become family. Hell, sometimes his mom called and didn't even ask to speak with Trevor—just Simon.

"Come on, let's get this stuff into the kitchen. The cake needs to go into the fridge. You can help me get the appetizers ready if you want," his mom told Simon.

"Hello? Did you forget about me? You know, the son you gave birth to," Trevor teased. He walked over and took the rest of the bags from her.

"Of course not, you big baby. Always wanting the attention." She smiled and gave Trevor a hug. "Now go, go. We have a lot to do before everyone arrives!"

"Always the slave-driver." Trevor playfully rolled his eyes before he, Simon, and his mom went into the kitchen he shared with Simon. Two months after he'd gotten out of rehab, he moved in officially.

"Where's your brother? He told me he was coming over early to help." Trevor's mom began emptying bags as Simon put the cake in the fridge.

"Oh, he came over early alright. He's out back on Trevor's bike. We can hardly keep him off the thing when he's here."

Trevor thought a lot while in rehab for the second time, about his life, what he had and what he wanted. He needed positive things in his world that he cared about. Yes, he had his family, Rock Solid, and Simon, but he needed some things that were just for him as well.

He'd gotten back into riding motocross and realized it was a good way to release stress. He tore up half of the back of their property riding, but it was one of the things he enjoyed most. As much as he loved Simon, Simon couldn't be everything to him, just like Trevor couldn't be everything to Simon. They loved each other—God, he loved the man so fucking much—but it was important for Trevor to live every aspect of his life, just as it was for Simon.

"I still don't think we need to have this party. I feel ridiculous." Simon looked over at Trevor, and Trevor smiled.

"Yes, we do. You not only wrote a book, but you sold it to a major publishing house. We need to have this party." Trevor pulled Simon over and kissed him.

"Okay, enough with that. Can you two help me? Everyone will be here soon." His mom tapped her foot, pretending to be annoyed.

"Are you sure you want our help? You've seen what we do in the kitchen," Simon told her.

She thought a minute. "You know what? You're right. Go make yourselves useful somewhere else. Send Jason in to help me when he gets here."

A few hours later, the lower floor of their house was full of people—some of Trevor's friends from his meetings, Alan and Heather, who were four months pregnant. The crew from Rock Solid were all there, Dr. Pham, and some more of Simon's colleagues from San Francisco, along with the staff from the small clinic that Simon had just opened in Rockford Falls. They'd only been in business a couple weeks. The process was longer than they'd realized, but Simon was an attending physician again.

Rock Solid picked up business in the past year as well. They still had a ways to go, but they had enough work to keep them all steady, which was what mattered.

"Hey, man. How's it going?" Blake nudged Trevor from behind as he watched Simon speaking with Heather.

"Good." He still couldn't believe this was his life sometimes. That he'd made it. It would be a battle forever. He knew that. But he'd made it.

"Things are going well with Simon's practice?" Blake asked.

"Yeah, it's good." He'd wondered in the beginning if Simon would miss San Francisco, if he would wish he'd gone back, but Trevor didn't think he did. Simon was happy. They both were.

"It's so strange to see you like this. Good, but weird. You did real good, big brother—your sobriety, your career, Simon. You did real good," he said again. "I'm proud of you."

Trevor would never get tired of hearing that. "Thanks, little brother. I couldn't do it without you." His brother, his best friend.

"Yeah, you could. But thanks. Have you seen Jason?"

"He's around here somewhere," Trevor replied. "He was on the front porch on his phone a little while ago."

Blake nodded and walked away to find Jason just as Simon headed toward Trevor. "I'm horny. Think we can sneak out of here without anyone noticing?" Trevor asked him, resulting in Simon grinning.

"I wish."

Trevor wrapped his arms around Simon. "I think you're enjoying this party more than you'd like to admit, Dr. Malone."

"Maybe I am." Simon fingered the coin on a chain around Trevor's neck. It was his coin for being two years sober. Simon wore Trevor's one year coin around his neck. "I'm a lucky man…I can't believe this is my life sometimes."

It didn't escape Trevor's attention that Simon used the same words Trevor had thought earlier. Neither could believe this was their life.

Simon tilted Trevor's face toward him and kissed him. "Thank you."

“For what?”

Simon shrugged. “Everything. For teaching me how to live. How to be happy.”

“I have to thank you for the same thing.”

They’d done that for each other—made each other happy. Things weren’t always easy, but what worth having really was? Trevor would always be a recovering addict…but the cravings were lessening. Being happy made things easier, having people he loved. He hadn’t had any close calls since that day in the hotel room. What mattered was that he kept fighting, kept trying, kept loving. That’s all life really was really about anyway. They had that, together.

“I want you. Sneak out with me. Live a little, doc. No one will notice we’re gone.”

Simon didn’t hesitate to do just what Trevor asked. They walked out together, knowing that for the first time in their lives, everything was rock solid.

Acknowledgment:

I'm blessed with the most incredible readers in the world. Thank you for always being there. My friends in the Riley's Rebels Facebook group, you make all my days brighter. Thanks for being rebels ☺ I'd like to thank all my beta readers, editors, proofreaders. You make my stories so much better.

About the Author:

Riley Hart is the girl who wears her heart on her sleeve. She's a hopeless romantic. A lover of sexy stories, passionate men, and writing about all the trouble they can get into together. If she's not writing, you'll probably find her reading.

Riley lives in California with her awesome family, who she is thankful for everyday.

You can find her online at:

Twitter

@RileyHart5

Facebook

https://www.facebook.com/riley.hart.1238?fref=ts

Blog

www.rileyhartwrites.blogspot.com

Other books by Riley Hart:

Broken Pieces

Full Circle

Losing Control

Blackcreek:

Collide

Stay

Pretend

Made in the USA
Monee, IL
07 June 2023